Belle Apocalypse

BY

LEE SIMPSON

Chapter One

'They're at it again !'

'Huh ?'

'Oh, sorry boss, didn't mean to wake you.'

'Who's at it again. Titans ?'

'No, no; the mortals. I've been watching the pool while you've been lying there asleep.'

Zeus slowly stretched himself, rubbed his eyes, sat up and let off a long loud yawn which, to his surprise, started off as a deep 'Moooo...' before this broke and turned into a groan. 'Ahhh.... my head, it feels like I've had stakes driven through my skull,' he exclaimed clutching at his forehead as if to grab something that wasn't there. 'What happened ?'

Hermes turned back to the pool and grinned to himself. 'You said you were getting bored with the French Revolution and were going out for a "bit of fun". You then turned yourself into a bull and made off with that dame Europa again. Boy, does she have an appetite for beef! Finally you dumped her on an island in the Mediterranean, came back up here and you've been asleep ever since. Never mind, I'll knock you up a potion, you'll feel right as rain.'

'So who's at it again. I hope all the gods have been obeying my instructions to stay out of the affairs of man. What's happened anyway in France. Have those sans-culottes guillotined the King and Queen yet ?'

Hermes was about to look a little sheepish, but given the king of the gods' recent penchant for animal impersonations thought better of it. 'Boss, I'm afraid you've been out for about a hundred years. The French Revolution ended long ago and I'm sorry to have to tell you this but whilst you've been out of the way the other gods have been running amok intervening all over the place down below.'

Zeus roused himself and shambled over to the pool. Hermes handed him the potion he had been preparing which the king of the gods quickly swallowed. He stared into the pool and as his head started to clear so did the image in the waters. 'So what's happening down there ?,' he said.

'Well,' started Hermes, who had been waiting to be asked, 'Europe; the continent named after your recent fling by the way; has continued to extend its rule over much of the rest of the world but remains bitterly divided itself. Shortly after you took your little nap a French general by the name of Napoleon came close to conquering the whole continent but he failed and since then, apart from the odd minor skirmish between individual states its been pretty quiet. There's a few small independent countries dotted around but the whole place is now largely dominated by six rival Great Powers.'

The King of the Gods zoomed in on the scene his messenger had been surveying and the sight astounded him. It was a naval dockyard in an estuary where the River Elbe joined the North Sea. A military band was playing. Bunting and flags fluttered in the breeze about a podium packed with dignitaries, some in top hats but most wearing spiked helmets and dressed in gaudy gold-braided uniforms of every description. Crowds thronged the jetties and surrounding riverbanks, cheering and waving as a gigantic battleship was launched down the slipway to crash into the water. When he had last inspected their activities mankind had nothing remotely like this. It was colossal, bristling with gun barrels port and starboard and with two huge gun turrets mounted fore and aft. Above all it seemed to be made entirely of solid steel. Miraculously it floated.

'Is that a metal battleship they have down there ?' asked an incredulous king of the gods.

'Yes boss, Poseidon was responsible for that.' said Hermes. 'They've all got them now.'

Zeus continued to watch as the monster ship, without the aid of a single sail, ploughed through the water towards an old wooden hulk lying moored about one mile off shore. As the ship turned alongside the hulk the gun barrels swivelled round and trained themselves on it. Then with a deafening roar they exploded their fire and fury on the hulk which was blasted into a thousand splinters in a matter of seconds. On the shore the crowds stamped and cheered their approval at this devastating spectacle.

'And what about those weapons. Who taught them how to make such powerful explosives ?' he demanded.

'That was Ares, boss,' said Hermes. 'Gunpowder's a thing of the past now. Some years ago he showed a Swedish chemist by the name of Nobel how to manufacture an explosive he called dynamite. With typical cynicism he persuaded the man that this would mean the end of all warfare since weapons would become so terrifying that nobody in their right minds would dream of using them.'

'I might have guessed. Well, go on,' said Zeus.

'Well boss, although there hasn't been a really big war for a long time, as you've noticed, they're all bristling to the brim down there with more powerful weapons than they've ever known or used before. It's been a powder keg waiting to blow for some time and now it looks like things are finally building up towards the big one, especially since Ares and Poseidon have been down there stirring it all up.'

'Those two again,' snapped Zeus, 'What exactly have they been up to?'

'Well, for some years now Ares has been posing as a Greek arms dealer going by the name of Basil Zararoff. He's been tremendously successful and has built up a huge fortune, first selling armaments to one power and then persuading their rivals of their need to catch up. Step by step the European powers have been steadily escalating the armed forces they all have pointing at each other which now run into millions of men.'

'Of all the gods Ares is the most odious to me since he enjoys nothing but strife, war and battles. What about old fishface ?' asked Zeus.

'Well he's been equally busy. He appeared in a dream to Kaiser Wilhelm of Germany promising him his favour, which persuaded the Kaiser to devote much his nation's military resources into building a huge battle fleet with which to challenge England's traditional domination of the seas. That's the Kaiser down there, by the way, the podgy one with the golden eagle on top of his helmet at the centre of the podium. Anyway, meanwhile the English public, whipped up by Poseidon, has demanded that their government build like crazy to stay ahead of the Germans.'

'So whilst Ares has been arming them to the teeth on land my brother has been ensuring that his realm is similarly equipped for the impending slaughter,' observed Zeus.

'Exactly boss' said Hermes.

Zeus studied the situation carefully. Everywhere he looked across the continent he could see soldiers, cavalrymen and sailors; guns, bombs and ships. Emperors and princelings strutted the world stage in fancy uniforms; reviewing troops here, inspecting armaments factories there, watching military exercises everywhere and forever huddled with generals discussing their plans for war against their neighbours.

'O.K. we're going to have to do something about this and pronto,' he finally said. 'I want you to summons a Council of the Gods. Let's see what Aries and Poseidon have got to say for themselves. Oh, and send in Ganymede on your way out.'

* * *

The Council of the Gods was Zeus' principle means of keeping in check the activities of all the other lesser deities. He would regularly call them together in the upper most chamber of Olympus and always start by tediously warning them in the most uncompromising terms of the fate that would befall any god or goddess foolish enough to set their will against his. This did from time to time happen but always to be followed by some terrible punishment. Even his wilful spouse Hera cautioned against the foolhardiness of openly defying Zeus from bitter personal experience.

In their heyday, whilst dining on ambrosia and quaffing their nectar, the gods had delighted in the fragrance of the fatted cattle being burnt in their honour by mortals drifting up from countless altars far below, but little of this went on anymore. They had been free as well to take sides in the quarrels of man but Zeus had severely curbed even this amusement after the Trojan War, of which the bitterness, rivalries and old scores to settle still obsessed many of them some three thousand years on.

As the gods had refrained from intervening in the affairs of the mortals so it seemed, over the millennia, mankind had turned its back on the gods. They now idled away the centuries in passive observation and the many lascivious distractions of Olympian life. Of course, not everyone was happy with this state of affairs and many yearned for the good old days to return, particularly Zeus' own brother Poseidon and the ever war-mongering Ares, but up until recently none had dared to openly challenge the boss' golden rule.

But it seemed that some had now taken the opportunity of Zeus' extended snooze to try and change things and the king of the gods knew that unless he nipped this in the bud pretty quickly the revolt might well spread.

In the marbled council chamber the gods chatted to each other whilst Hebe passed round golden goblets of nectar and little sausages on sticks, which had proved a very popular substitute for the smell of sacrificial offerings. Zeus and Hermes watched them through the curtains.

'I wish Hercules would learn to leave his club and that mangy old lion skin outside when he comes here. And Artemis' bloody dogs are trying to get at the sausages. No sign of Poseidon or Ares then ?,' said Zeus.

'They're determined to go all the way on this one boss. I didn't think they'd show. I finally tracked them down conferring together in a cave in the Alps. Ares reckons they've already stirred up things so much that nothing you can do is now going to stop the nations of Europe from rushing headlong into war with each other. He's ready to glory in the slaughter of millions of soldiers across the battlefields of Europe whilst Poseidon is slavering at the thought of all those poor sailors being sent to the depths of his realm.' Hermes replied.

'O.K. Get out there and announce me.'

Hermes walked out to the podium. 'Testing, 1,2,3,4..... Divinities, may I please have your attention and a big round of applause for the king of the gods, Zeus.'

Zeus appeared from behind the drapes. 'As you know, I've been asleep for the past 100 years. And not one of you buggers had the grace to wake me up! I know, all too busy intervening in the affairs of man when I wasn't looking, and look what a mess you've all made of it down there. Meanwhile I've missed the French Revolution, the Crimean War, the rise of Germany, even the bloody American Civil War. Well fortunately for you lot Hermes had the good sense to record it all, so I can at least catch up.'

'Anyway, we'll come back to that later. You'll notice that two of your number are missing and I don't think there's too many surprises around here at what they've been up to. Ares and Poseidon have been manipulating the leaders of the major European powers who are now rushing towards all out war with each other. Millions of mortals stand to be slaughtered. Now, as you all know, I don't normally like our intervening in the affairs of man; apart from the odd bit of fun that is; but since Ares and Poseidon are behind this in the first place I feel it incumbent on us to try to do something to prevent the coming mayhem.'

'So what I'd like to do is this. I want one god to take special responsibility for each of the six leaders of the Great Powers, to get down there fast, and then do everything you can to prevent your man from going to war. If minor wars between individual powers have already started then do your best to get them resolved before they lead to a major conflagration. So, who want's which leader ?'

A buzz of conversation started up amongst the gods. 'Come on,' bellowed Zeus, 'let's have some volunteers.'

Finally the crowd parted as the massive figure of Hercules walked up to the podium. Seven foot tall, long black flowing beard, bristling with muscles and clenching a giant wooden club larger than a man, he stood naked but for the lion skin draped over his shoulder.

'Kaiser Wilhelm of Germany,' boomed Hercules, 'He's my sort of man; big, strong, an athlete through and through. I'll take him.' Hermes stifled a mischievous smile.

'O.K. fine. Hercules gets the Kaiser,' agreed Zeus, 'Now, who'll take Tsar Nicholas of Russia.

'Me.' said a voice from the back, and the beautiful but terrifying figure of Athena, wearing a long flowing toga and helmet, carrying her huge spear and shield, moved forward. 'Tsar Nicholas is so wise, a patron of the arts and sciences. I will look over his fortunes.' she said.

'Right, that's two.' said Zeus. 'Who wants the Austrian Emperor Franz Josef ?'

'I'll take the Hapsburg Emperor.' It was the soft, beguiling voice of the beautiful Artemis, her long brown hair flowing over a short belted tunic, carrying her bow and quiver of arrows, whilst her two hounds stood guard by her sandaled feet, snarling at any gods who moved too close to their mistress. 'Franz Josef is so swift and deadly. I look forward to getting to know him better.'

'O.K. any callers for President Loubet of France,' said Zeus.

'The French are such wonderful lovers and none among them has a higher reputation in this field than their President. I think its now time for Emile Loubet to learn the real meaning of making love and not war.' Aphrodite herself had deigned to select the French President on whom to visit an ecstasy rarely known by mortal man. 'Junior, pack your bow and arrows. Sounds like we're gonna need them,' she called to a small winged child who had been hovering nearby. Hermes shot a sniggering glance at Apollo, who had been busily chatting up the goddess of love during the reception, and Apollo glowered angrily back at him.

'Four down, two to go,' said Zeus. 'Anyone want the English Prime Minister Salisbury ?'

'This England seems a green and fertile land and their Prime Minister is an industrious and hard working servant of the people. Above all, and unlike some people I could name around here, they know how to respect royalty. I would like to visit this island.' It was Zeus' own wife Hera, the Queen of the Gods, her mature, stern and beautiful face veiled beneath a diademed head and dressed in a long blue tunic adorned with peacock feathers.

'Right, that just leaves Turkey,' said Zeus, 'Who will take the Sultan Abdul Hamid ?'

There was a shuffle of conversation and then a silence.

'C'mon, c'mon, one of the rest of you has got to take Turkey,' Zeus demanded.

'Well hopefully this won't take too long and since I am, among other things, the god of medicine I might as well attend to the "sick man of Europe",' said Apollo. 'Hopefully at least I'll have time to practise my lyre and roger a few of the Sultan's odalisques before the Austrian and Russian armies get to them all first.'

'Right, that's that decided,' declared Zeus.

'What about Italy, boss,' said Hermes. 'I don't mind taking Italy.'

'No,' said Zeus, 'Italy doesn't figure as a Great Power and anyway I need you for other things.'

Hermes looked a little downcast, fearing he was going to miss out on the fun.

'You stay here, Hermes. The rest of you are dismissed. And I want regular reports on your progress. Remember, you have each been assigned a mortal who controls one of the six Great Powers who are all poised to rush into a devastating war with each other which could spell the end of civilisation. Its up to you to use your special powers on your chosen man to prevent this.'

As the gods shuffled out Zeus drew Hermes to one corner and put a bulky arm across his slender shoulders. 'Don't think I can trust any of them to play it straight,' he whispered. 'They've all got their own axes to grind and I know them all well enough to know that they will play out their rivalries with each other through the fortunes of their chosen mortal; giving assistance here, sending a calamity there, you know the sort of thing.'

'Then why did you send them on their missions to prevent a headlong rush into world war if, by the sound of things, you think they're only going to make matters worse ?' asked his baffled assistant.

'Because, you dimwit, somebody left me sleeping for one hundred bloody years and I missed the Napoleonic Wars, which I'd been looking forward to ever since the start of the French Revolution. I know you recorded it but that's never the same as watching it live. Anyway, it seems at least I've woken up just in the nick of time to catch this one, which looks like its going to be a goody, and if by letting that mob loose on those six fools down below that helps to spice things up a bit then it should be even more entertaining. Meanwhile this way I can keep better track on them and know what they're all up to whilst I take care of Ares and Poseidon'. Zeus revealed his master plan to his trusted messenger. 'Now I want you to get down there and keep me regularly posted on what those six buggers are doing.'

'I get it, boss. Brilliant !' said Hermes as the penny dropped. 'What about the mortals though, all those millions of soldiers, sailors and civilians who are going to perish ?'

'Screw 'em. That's their problem,' replied the king of the gods.

* * *

After the meeting Artemis, Athena and Hera stopped off in the ladies' washroom.

'Huh,' Athena snorted. 'Well girls, what are we going to do about this. We can't risk letting that brazen hussy outshine any of us by promoting the fortunes of the Frenchman. Paris, of all the places she's off to. Paris ! The name of that fool of a shepherd that she conned into awarding her the golden apple which started all that Trojan War business in the first place. Hera, your man doesn't sound too bad; industrious, hardworking; can you get him to attack the French.'

'Industrious, hardworking ! Don't make me laugh,' laughed Hera. 'I only said that for the old man's benefit. Lord Salisbury is the archetypal English aristocrat; y'know, a fag at Eton and a spell in the Guards preparing gin and tonics for royalty before taking up his rotten borough seat in Parliament at twenty-three and then his hereditary country seat on the death of his father. Foreign policy is his one big political interest and the preservation of peace by maintaining what he calls a "balance of power" between the big nations.'

'Oh dear,' said Athena, 'that doesn't sound very promising if we want to stop Aphrodite showing off her latest mortal patsy. What about your man, Art, the Austrian Emperor. "Swift and deadly" you said.'

'Sorrrrrry...,' said the goddess of the hunt. 'Likewise I only said that for Zeus' benefit. Have you ever seen Emperor Franz Josef ?. Firstly, he's over seventy years old with great bushy sideburns. About the only thing he's ever likely to catch is going to be pneumonia. Plus, he's totally indecisive. He'd like to reassert the once great Hapsburg Empire, but he rules over a patchwork quilt of rebellious would-be nations and has long since lost leadership of the Teutonic peoples to Germany. Not a lot of hope there I'm afraid, but what about your man; wise, a patron of the arts and sciences ?'

'Er, well, yes. It seems I too have a confession to make,' said Athena. 'Tsar Nicholas is actually a morose inadequate whose one great ambition in life is to maintain the divine and absolute authority of the crown. He in turn is ruled over by his wife who in her turn is infatuated with one fortune teller, soothsayer or bogus holy man after the other. The Russians have had an obsessive compulsion to defend themselves by continuously expanding their frontiers but they're now contained by rival powers on all sides and the country is too poor and backward to effectively challenge any of its neighbours.'

'It doesn't look like we've got very promising material to work with then by the sound of things,' said Hera, 'but I suppose we're going to have to do what we can. Unfortunately my man Salisbury looks like he's making every effort to be pally with the Frenchman and is more concerned about the German naval build up and Russian interference on the north-west frontier of India.'

'Well that's another good point.' said Artemis, 'I'm sure between us we can keep the English and the Russians apart but neither do we want to see old muscle-brains' man do well, unless of course he attacks the French. Unlike our bunch of losers, this Kaiser Wilhelm sounds like he could be a force to be reckoned with and much more promising material to work with. How in Hades did Hercules manage to have the sense to grab him first ?'

'Who knows ?,' said Hera, 'Anyway, we better not hang around here too long. Walls have ears. The first thing we'd better do is pay a visit to our respective charges and see what we can do to put a bit of fire in their bellies. We'll meet up again later and discuss things further.'

With that the goddess of wisdom headed for the Tsar's Palace in St Petersburg, the goddess of the hunt zeroed in on the Hapsburg Emperor's private clinic in the Austrian Alps, whilst the queen of the gods got lost in Hertfordshire and had to ask a policeman the way to Hatfield House.

* * *

'Hey, baby, wait up. Where you going in such a hurry ?,' Apollo called out to Aphrodite on the path down from Olympus.

Aphrodite stopped and turned to him. 'Not now honey,' she said, 'You were in there, you know the score, we haven't got a lot of time to prevent the whole of Europe going up in flames.'

'Aahhh Shhheeeeeettt......,' scoffed Apollo, 'You don't really believe all that bull the old man was just spurting out, do you ?. Anyway, what is it with this Loubet dude anyhow. I thought you'n me had something going. I swear you let him lay one finger on you and I'll turn him into a frog, stick a tube up his arse and blow him into the Atlantic Ocean.'

'Why Apollo,' gasped Aphrodite, 'I do believe your jealous.'

Apollo looked a little red faced and picked at the strings of his lyre uneasily.

'Anyway honey,' she said, 'you got nothing to worry about over ol' President Emile Loubet. That what I told the boss man, about him being a big stud an' all, well, I was just making that up. Sure he keeps up a big front with lots a beautiful women in different apartments around Paris, that's the only way a politician can get elected by the penis-brained French, but in reality he's totally impotent, he can't do a thing with it.'

'So what you gonna do with him now,' asked Apollo, 'You can't afford to let him go under to either Athena or Hera's men. They'd never let you live it down after that Judgement of Paris stunt you pulled on them.'

'I know,' replied Aphrodite. 'Trouble is he won't bite the bullet and attack anyone. He want's France to be the world's leading power but he's terrified of Germany. How about your man, the Sultan, can he help ?'

'I doubt it,' said Apollo. 'I only picked him because I thought it looks like he's not going to last very long anyway and I could get back to doing something useful. The Ottoman Empire has been falling apart for decades and is now only being held together because the other powers couldn't agree on who'd get what bit next. Still, things can always change so I suppose I'd better get down there and have a look around Turkey. I'm sure the place must have some delights and it would be nice to visit Troy again.'

'O.k. honey, anyway I gotta get to Paris. Eros is waiting for me down the path. We'll catch up with each other soon' said Aphrodite, and with that she blew him a kiss and left.

'Always got to have the brat in tow with her,' thought Apollo, and he sat down to sing a song on his lyre.

Suddenly the ground began to tremble as a gigantic figure dressed only in a lion skin and wielding a huge wooden club came thundering down the path his face scowling.

'Hey up, big fella, gimme five,' called out Apollo.

'Huh ?,' said Hercules.

'Where you going dude ?,' said Apollo.

'Berlin,' snapped back Hercules.

'Jeeez...,' thought Apollo, 'having a conversation with this guy is like watching milk curdle, but he seems a little unhappy about something.'

'So you seem to have picked a winner with the Kaiser then, eh,' ventured Apollo, trying to make conversation.

'Grrrr..,' growled Hercules, 'its that little shit Hermes playing tricks again. If I get my hands on him I'll pull his head off.'

'Join the queue,' said Apollo, 'so what's he done now ?'

'He told me Kaiser Wilhelm was a big, strong athlete, like me.'

'And...?'

'I've been checking. It seems he's a flabby, flatulent deviant who only spends so much time in the men's' gymnasium and steam room because..., because....., no, its too terrible to say. And that little bastard Hermes is responsible for me being sent to him.'

Apollo inwardly chuckled to himself but was all sympathy to the angry giant standing before him. 'Anyway, your man's got a big fleet that Poseidon persuaded him to build. Can't you get him to attack the English with it,' he asked.

'Maybe,' said Hercules, 'Like a spoiled brat demanding attention he keeps provoking one international crisis after another and then humiliates himself and his nation by having to climb down. Sooner or later though he's likely to push things to far.'

'Interesting,' thought Apollo to himself, 'From what I've learned today I'm not sure the old man was right when he thought war was inevitable between the European powers. Still, I suppose we can soon make sure that it is.'

'Anyway Butch, good luck in the steam bath and watch where you stick that mighty club of yours,' Apollo called to Hercules, making an obscene gesture with his arm. Hercules angrily swung his great club but the god of light was gone in a flash.

* * *

Chapter Two

The brilliant evening sunshine cast its shadows over the city of light in the first spring of the first year of a beautiful new age. To the aristocrats and the artists, the writers, the poets and the glamorous women from across the world who flocked to Paris everything about this city represented the glorious peak of human civilisation that had arrived with the twentieth century. An age where science, industry and enlightened government at last promised to free mankind from the drudgery of toil, disease, want and war.

Under the towering gaze of Eiffel's great steel monument to the age of industry, completed just eleven years earlier, gaily coloured crowds thronged the bright, wide boulevards that the self-appointed Emperor Napoleon III had created after bulldozing the old narrow streets and slums of the medieval city centre to deter the Parisian's passion for barricade building and to allow his cavalry room to swiftly put down any challenge to his imperial rule. Both Louis Napoleon and his short-lived Second Empire had been swept away by the war with Prussia of 1871. In its place was proclaimed the French Third Republic from the besieged capital. From the occupied French palace of Versailles, the Second Reich was also proclaimed. A new unified German Empire under Prussian leadership, forged by this last of Bismarck's wars from the patchwork of independent petty German states that since the days of Richelieu it had been the cornerstone of French foreign policy to prevent ever coming into being.

Over the following decades France had flourished and the open air theatres of the city entertaining the new bourgeois and the sans-coulettes alike attested to the wealth and wonders of the Republic's growing overseas Empire with huge decorative motifs modelled on the exotic beasts and the architecture of Africa, Asia and the far Pacific. But the new giant on her eastern border had grown ever stronger threatening to far outstrip France in her industrial and economic power, her manpower and her military strength, making the prospect of ever fulfilling 'la revanche'; redress for the German annexation of the French provinces of Alsace and Lorraine at the end of the war; an ever more distant dream.

As the chimes of the nearby Notre Dame cathedral echoed over the multi coloured masses below they mingled with the beams of light which pierced through the shuttered windows of an Isle St Louis apartment to illuminate like a zebra a naked white-haired man with an immaculately trimmed moustache and beard as he stepped from his bath.

President Emile Loubet of the French Third Republic looked down at his withered willy and sighed.

'C'est la vie,' he thought to himself, 'If only once I could feel some stirring below, if only once I could really take one of these beauties, that I am forced to conduct this charade with, into my arms and stick it to her, like a real Frenchman would do. But alas, I am condemned to this awful fate. Once a week to spend an hour in some dingy apartment with a glamour girl with whom I can do nothing, simply so word of my paramours can be spread. Nothing overtly in the press of course, just a sly wink here and a nod there from those who think they're in the know. And my glorious political career must hang on my reputation as the greatest lover in all of France. Oh what cruel destiny !'

'Still,' he thought, 'at least it gives me a chance to get some peace and quiet away from this damned Dreyfus business and to concentrate on building the alliance against Germany.'

A few years earlier France, the only Republic amongst the European powers, had formed an unlikely alliance with Russia, the most autocratic and despotic of them. Recovery of Alsace and Lorraine was fast starting to take second place in French concerns to the prospect of a new German invasion but the alliance with Russia appeared more aimed at Great Britain than Germany. Russia herself had little quarrel with Germany but England seemed everywhere determined to halt the Tsar's ambitions to extend his empire in the east in what to them was the "Great Game". Meanwhile, try as they might to avoid it, the French couldn't help clashing with England as the two nations sought to further the interests of their own colonial empires. Loubet, and his Foreign Minister Delcassé, were desperate to bring the English into a more determinedly anti-German alliance but these constant colonial disputes, the most recent of which had been an argument over whose flag should flutter above a dilapidated Sudanese fortress in a place called Fashoda; which previously scarcely a single Englishman or Frenchman had ever heard of; and the subsequent French climb down had humiliated French honour and inflamed public opinion against their old colonial rival.

As he donned his robe he wondered what this latest girl would be like. Marcel, his procurer of discreet, beautiful women who liked to make an easy Franc, had never been more enthusiastic about a girl before. 'A fat lot of good that's going to do me,' thought Loubet. 'I hope she can at least boil an egg or something.'

He opened the bathroom door and walked into the lounge where the girl was sitting cross legged on the sofa. Loubet was suddenly frozen to the spot at the sight of her. Everything about the girl was exquisite. Her long blonde hair flowing over her tanned Mediterranean shoulders. Her full, ample breasts softly and visibly heaving beneath a thin chiffon vest. Two eyes like deep blue whirlpools turned to him and the soft red lips parted as if in some whispered command.

He felt a sudden stitch in his heart, a cloud of camembert washed through his brain, and he found himself falling to the carpet in slow motion. As his mind cleared he looked up and there was the girl bending over him offering him a glass of strange bubbling liquid.

'Here, Monsieur President, drink this,' she whispered as she handed him the glass.

Her voice was like a thousand violins vibrating in every cell of his body. As he looked into her eyes he cried with the pain of such perfect beauty, as if staring into the sun. 'Drink,' she said again softly, and without further thought Loubet downed the draft.

'Here, come and sit with me on the sofa and tell me what sort of day you've had,' she said, patting the seat by her side. Loubet pulled himself up and sat down next to her, his head still spinning. Then, as he sat, still trying to comprehend the girl's incredible beauty, a strange thing started to happen. At first imperceptible, he thought he felt a slight movement under his bathrobe. He looked down. Sure enough, it was starting to move by itself. He gazed in amazement as the bulge in the towelling grew ever larger and a strange sensation he had never felt before came over him.

Loubet leapt up, rushed into the bathroom and flung off the bathrobe.

'YYYYeeeeeessssssssssssss !!!!!. YYYYessss !!!!. Its like a steel girder !' he screamed in excitement and triumph from behind the bathroom door.

A few seconds later Loubet emerged from the bathroom with a champagne bucket carefully concealing the still throbbing bulge in his bathrobe whilst nonchalantly dangling two glasses from his other hand.

'How's about you and I repair to the other room, mon cheri,' he crooned, trying to imitate how he thought the great lovers of the opera sounded.

'Not so fast buster,' said the girl, 'they said I only had to chat, maybe boil you an egg or something. They never said nothing 'bout no nookie.'

'But my dear,' said Loubet, somewhat taken by surprise at this rejection, 'this is Paris, the night was made for love, and we are two beautiful love birds. What else should we do.'

'Well, we could talk about your plans to invade England,' said the girl.

'My whattt ...?' screamed Loubet, dumbfounded, and then, 'Oh no !' as he started to feel a slight ebbing.

'Your plans to invade England,' repeated the girl, 'Surely you're not going to let the humiliating climb down France was forced to suffer last year over Fashoda go unavenged.'

'But England isn't the threat,' squealed Loubet. 'I don't want to attack England. I'm trying to persuade England to join our alliance with Russia against Germany.' Loubet's desperation grew as he felt a further slackening below. 'You don't want to worry your pretty little head about things like that.'

'But if you don't attack England now, then surely the day will come when England will overrun France. I could never love a man who would leave poor French virgins like myself to the mercy of the vile English invaders,' she replied with her face full of helplessness and fear at the awful prospect.

'Mon Dieu, she's a virgin,' thought Loubet. 'Please mon cheri, I'll think about it, I promise, now please, please, can we go into the bedroom,' he pleaded.

'And what about the Suez Canal ?,' she asked.

'Huh !!?' Then Loubet felt yet another loosening in the exquisite tautness between his legs. 'What about the frigging Suez Canal,' he screamed.

'Well, we French built it and then let the English steal it from under our nose. French dignity requires that we seize back the Suez Canal,' she insisted.

'O.K., O.K., I'll attack England. I'll take back the Suez Canal. Oh no....!'

'What's the matter honey ?'

'Nothing, nothing. Please mon cheri, into the bedroom. QUICKLY !'

'And Russia ?'

'Yes, yes, I'll attack Russia as well,' he sobbed, not quite bothering to consider just how this might be achieved with Germany lying in between. 'Anything, anything. Just please, into the bedroom now.'

But it was too late, the moment had passed.

'Hey that's kind of a shame, honey. You seem to have gone all floppy again,' said the girl. 'Still, not to worry. We're going to need to work on this thing a little more if you're really going to be able to keep it up long enough, in both senses, to use it properly. But never fear, we'll get there in the end. Well, I guess my time's up for now. I'm due to see you again next week and I'll look forward to hearing all about your plans for licking them wicked English. I'm sure that if you can thrill me with tales of French military daring do, then I can find a way to thrill you. Till then, you take care d'you hear.'

And with that the girl, who's name he still didn't know, got up and left.

President Loubet wept.

* * *

In the weeks that followed Paris experienced something of a summer of love as the influence of Aphrodite and her mischievous offspring's presence were felt. Aphrodite became the toast of the bohemian society. Artists painted her pictures, poets wrote sonnets to her, musicians composed operas in her honour and sculptors wondered at the remarkable similarity between this beauty and the armless treasure of the Louvré museum. As his mother slept away the days and partied into the night Eros roamed the city loosing his bolts with gay abandon.

Once a week she kept her appointment with the President and Loubet lived for this moment from one minute to the next. There they would discuss his plans for an invasion of England and work on the President's little problem to the point where the two projects had become synonymous and inter-related ambitions in his mind. Just as much careful planning and preparation was necessary in order to mount a successful invasion of the British Isles so, the girl explained, would be required much time, work and effort before the President would be able to achieve a valid and sustainable erection. But rest assured, she had promised him, that day would come. Then and only then would she and her heroic French conqueror be able to know true union. The very thought filled Loubet with ecstasy and spurred him into determination to achieve success in both undertakings.

Aphrodite had prescribed for the President a rigorous course of mental and physical exercises which included five minutes of intensive massaging of the organ regularly throughout the day, seven days a week. In truth she had the power to turn on and turn off the poor man's erection at will but she needed to stretch the thing out until the invasion of England was irrevocably underway and her humiliation of her old rival Hera, the queen of the gods, assured. Anyway, the thought of the President's exertions gave her mild amusement.

As ever, Loubet's thoughts were on the girl as the members of his government and the Chiefs of Staff convened in the council chamber of the Elyseé Palace to approve their secret plans for waging war on England. Loubet had long since failed to give any consideration as to the "why" France should want to go to war with England. Only the "how" concerned him now and the need to carry his government with him. The latter had proven surprisingly easy. Of course the Anglophile Foreign Minister Delcassé had demurred but he had been isolated and intimidated into silence by the general enthusiasm shown by other government ministers who, considering how popular such an adventure would be with a French electorate still outraged by the previous year's humiliation over Fashoda and the huge profits to be made when France stripped England of her colonies in East Africa and her influence in Egypt, had eagerly backed the idea.

A general had been summing up the huge numerical superiority the French army held over the British, more than double their numbers and with Britain's forces anyway widely dispersed around the world and heavily committed in South Africa and India.

'Yes, yes. That's all well and good,' Delcassé ventured one last attempt to inject some sanity into the proceedings. 'But aren't you missing one important little point. The French army is in France. How are we supposed to get our forces across the channel to engage the English when the Royal Navy controls the sea. Our armies may well dwarf those of the English but our navy cannot possibly challenge theirs. Our forces would be destroyed before they'd even catch sight of the white cliffs of Dover.'

Loubet simply smiled. 'Send in Monsieur Blanc,' he called.

A diminutive, frock-coated figure entered the chamber to stand before the assembled ministers and generals.

'Gentlemen, may I present Monsieur Henri le Blanc, the finest civil engineer in all of France, and therefore naturally anywhere in the world,' Loubet beamed.

'Monsieur le Blanc,' said Loubet, 'would you please explain to the Foreign Minister and the other gentlemen here just how exactly we will transport the French army across the English Channel.'

'Certainly, Monsieur President,' the moustachioed little man replied. 'We will not go across the Channel. We will go underneath it, in a tunnel.'

Chapter Three

Slowly, above and around the darkened courtyards and minarets of the Imperial Palace, St. Petersburg an owl silently glided, perching occasionally on a ledge and staring in through the windows as if searching for something. Splendid gilt, tapestries, furniture, paintings, statues and opulence of every kind adorned the empty corridors and chambers of the palace but it seemed the owl could not find what she was looking for. Finally its keen ears picked up a faint sound of music drifting from a distant and remote tower of the palace from which gleamed a faint light. The owl silently flapped its wings, lifted into the air and headed for the tower.

On landing on the ledge and peering through the window into a dim, candle lit hall, the owl glimpsed a disgusting spectacle. Rotted food, stale alcohol and even less palatable waste was everywhere beneath and atop coarse wooden tables and benches set on cold stone floors; in stark contrast to the scenes elsewhere in the palace. Minstrels, revellers, serving wenches and animals roamed about haphazardly. A tall priest with long straggly black hair reclined in a huge wooden bath tub accompanied by three young girls who were trying to clean something from his filthy beard. A dwarf danced on a table whilst playing a tune on an accordion, surrounded by laughing, naked girls who were tugging at his britches. Astronomers huddled in one corner arguing over their charts. On another table alchemists mixed potions from bubbling phials to be eagerly consumed by the debauchees.

The owl studied the sickening scene below her with revulsion. It was the very antithesis of everything she stood for. Culture, science, virtue and chastity were all being trashed underfoot in this orgy of superstition, degradation and excess; and at the very heart of the Tsar's Imperial Palace. She noted every face and was at least a little relieved not to find the one she searched for amongst this sorry throng. But where was he ?

On the far side of the palace stood another tower where she thought she caught a faint flickering of a candle-lit shadow against the window. The owl again took to the air.

Finally, through the grimy window, the owl saw him. It was a small, austere private office, adorned only by a few grim icons and crosses around the walls and illuminated by a single candlestick atop an ornate desk. A bottle of wine had been toppled and the remains of its contents were dribbling out over some papers and were starting to stain red the gold-braided sleeve of Tsar Nicholas II as he slumped forward on the desk sobbing, 'Oh Alex. My poor, dear, brave Alex.'

'Hades,' thought the owl, 'this is going to be more difficult than I thought. How am I ever going to get through to this creature. He's too sodden to try reasoning with and too morose to try seducing.'

As she watched a uniformed aide entered the room and gingerly approached the desk, righting the wine bottle and gently daubing at the Tsar's stained sleeve with a silk handkerchief.

'Your Majesty, please, you must go to bed and get some rest and then get cleaned up before the visit of the Austrian ambassador tomorrow,' pleaded the flunky.

'Le'me alone,' moaned the Tsar. 'Ge'me another drink. Go away.'

'Majesty, please,' the flunky persisted.

'She's a shaint, Igor,' whimpered the Tsar, 'an absholute shaint. Do you know what she has to go through? Night after night with her holy men in prayer and devotions all for the sake of our poor little Tsaravitch Alexei.'

Tsar Nicholas rolled over and spewed, most of which ended up down his other sleeve. Then helped by the exasperated flunky he slowly rose to unsteady feet.

'Majesty, let me help you to your bedchamber,' said the servant.

'Get off me,' repeated the Tsar, and let off a belch. 'Just give me a candle, I can find my own bloody way to bed. Who'd you think I am anyway. Some helpless child. Well I'm the Rah of all the Zushas, just don't you forget that.' And so saying he staggered away towards his bedchamber.

Nicholas stumbled down a long dark stone corridor illuminated only by his candle. Up a flight of stone steps, along another corridor, down a flight of steps, along another corridor. He started to feel uneasy. Surely he should have reached his bedchamber by now. And why hadn't he passed any palace guards? The place seemed deserted. Suddenly a gust of wind extinguished his candle. He was plunged into darkness, but for a faint glow of moonlight coming from a bend in the corridor ahead. Sweat broke out on the Tsar's forehead as he realised the moonlight was casting a eerie shadow of a figure standing in the corridor beyond the bend.

'Who's there,' his voice croaked meekly.

'Golubchik, is that you,' came the reply.

'Golubchik ???,' thought the Tsar, 'That voice, no it can't be, it can't be....' 'MOTHER !,' he yelled and ran towards figure.

There before him stood his mother. The Tsarina Maria Fedorova. Five foot tall, dumpy, those stern features staring out from a shock of grey hair beneath her favourite diamond tiara. Just as he remembered her; before she died in 1883.

'My son,' said the spectre, 'Look how you disgrace the Romanov name, and bring shame on our house with your superstitions and your debauched carrying on.'

Tears flowed down the Tsar's face. 'Mother, I'm sorry. I'm so sorry. I'll stop it. Now. Forever. I promise you mother, only please don't leave me again,' he sobbed.

'Worst of all though....,' continued the apparition.

'Anything, mother. I'll do anything you say,' wept the Tsar.

'...you are leaving Mother Russia at the mercy of the foreign enemies.'

'Eh ?,' Nicholas exclaimed, 'But mother, the Empire has never been greater. We are at peace with all the other powers and I've just agreed an alliance with France against the threat of Germany.'

'Golubchick, you're a fool and will always be a fool,' the old woman scoffed. 'France is the real enemy you have to fear. How can you, the absolute ruler of your people by the divine grace of God, side with those rabble rousing proletariat republican scum. You must attack France now before its too late.'

'Attack France ?,' squealed the baffled Tsar. 'But mother, we're not anywhere near France. We don't have any borders with them. How can I attack them, we'd have to travel through Germany first ?'

'Well, er, all right then,' said the Tsarina's ghost. 'You'd better attack Germany first then. But don't take your eye off France at all.'

'But mother,' persisted the Tsar. 'I can't attack Germany without French help. They're too strong.'

'Listen to your mother son,' she said in a stern voice. 'Either you attack France when they're not expecting it, or they'll be attacking you when you are least ready for it.'

'How about if I try to get France to attack Germany and then stay out of it myself,' he asked.

'Forget it son, you're not smart enough,' was his mother's dismissive reply.

Nicholas started thinking frantically. He knew he had to obey his mother and attack France but he couldn't risk plunging Russia into a war with Germany simply in order to give him a route to France. Then inspiration struck.

'Turkey !,' he cried, 'I'll attack Turkey. France fought with us when we attacked Turkey in grandfather's time. If we attack Turkey again maybe the French will come and attack us again but this time we'll be ready for them. England as well if need be.'

'Hmmm.., Apollo.' the ghost pondered, making a reference which Nicholas didn't understand. 'That doesn't sound too bad. O.k., you attack Turkey first but if France doesn't then come to you I expect you to use the new found access you'll get to the Mediterranean to launch an invasion of the French Riviera.'

The Tsar nodded fervently in agreement, inwardly beaming that his mother had actually approved of one of his suggestions.

'And now my son, it is time for me to return to the twilight world,' she said.

'Mother, please stay,' yelled the Tsar.

'I can't, but if you do as I say and attack Russia's enemies, then I may be able to return to see you again soon. Will you do that for your poor old mother son ?' she asked, as her image slowly started to shimmer and fade.

'I will mother, I promise,' cried the Tsar. And the ghost of the Tsarina Maria Fedorova was gone.

'Funny,' Nicholas thought to himself, 'She was never that interested in foreign affairs when she was alive. And I thought she always quite liked France.'

* * *

Chapter Four

Kaiser Wilhelm II was very excited. After months of preparation the day had finally arrived. Today was going to be a great day when he was going to pull his greatest ever stunt. No matter how many times he thought about it he never failed to giggle in anticipation. He had even arranged for new cinematographic cameras to be on hand to record the event and he looked forward to playing the scenes back endlessly to his amused courtiers and their peels of laughter.

Wilhelm winced as the valet made another turn of the handle on the contraption that tightened the corset, dragging and holding in place the mounds of unsightly flesh which would otherwise mar the Kaiser's athletic appearance befitting of a Prussian officer.

'What time is the train due ?' he eagerly asked the valet, although he knew full well.

'3 pm, Majesty,' the valet replied.

'Have you laid out my tallest platform boots ?'

'Yes Majesty.'

'Is everything else laid on ?,' he asked.

'Yes Majesty.'

Now King Umberto of Italy was of very diminutive stature and Wilhelm, who was quite tall himself, privately referred to him as 'the dwarf'. Because of his sensitivity about his height the Italian King had long made a habit of recruiting only the very shortest members of the Italian army to his Royal Bodyguard, who accompanied the King everywhere he went. This all worked perfectly well in Italy where every public engagement was carefully orchestrated but today the King was arriving in Berlin for an official state visit. For the last six months the Kaiser had been combing the vast German armed forces for only the very tallest soldiers to recruit to his Imperial Bodyguard.

For the thousandth time, Wilhelm chuckled again with laughter at the thought of the scene that was due to take place at Berlin's Lehrter Banhnhof that afternoon when, in all their finery, the tiny Italian King and his diminutive bodyguard would step off the train to be greeted by the lofty Kaiser and his retinue of German giants. Tears rolled down his face as he imagined the little Italian guardsmen darting around like comic pigmies between the legs of the towering German supermen and the embarrassment of the Italian King.

'Well, Otto,' the Kaiser beamed as he stared in the mirror at his fine figure, courtesy of the corset, 'I think after breakfast I'll have a little work out in the military gymnasium and then perhaps a spell in the steam baths to ready myself for this afternoon's fun.'

* * *

Heracles had changed his lion skin into a huge white bath towel. Fortunately it was customary and considered manly for the German servicemen, who were given free access to the facilities by gracious decree of the Kaiser, to go about their exercises and training at the gymnasium totally naked, so he hoped he wouldn't look too out of place. He had changed his giant club to look like one of those tiny wooden rods with small balls of cotton wool stuck to both ends which he had seen lying around about the place, and he was standing by a shower bench staring at the rod and wondering how it was supposed to be used.

'Fritz, who is that man ?,' the Kaiser called to the gymnasium manager.

'Which man Majesty ?,' came the reply.

'That one, that absolute giant over there poking his little cotton wool dibble up his bottom. I like that in a man, by the way. Shows concern for all round cleanliness. Make a note. I'd like to see more of that around here.' The Kaiser pointed Heracles out to the gym manager.

'Oh him. I don't know Majesty other than that he's some country boy squaddie. He turned up this morning and has just about worn out every piece of equipment in the gym. He's been lifting weights more than double the records set in the Olympic Games.'

'What, ' gasped Wilhelm, 'That's incredible. Hey, you there. Yes. you. Come over here.'

Heracles looked up to see a pink, flabby figure wrapped in a bath towel and wearing on his head an ornate gilt helmet mounted by a golden spread eagle beckoning to him. He pounded over.

Wilhelm looked him up and down, those mighty biceps, those powerful thighs, that huge slab of manhood and, above all, that towering height, many inches taller than Wilhelm's tallest guardsman. He had never seen such a perfect example of a Teutonic superman before and he resolved there and then that this individual would be leading his Imperial Guard when he greeted the Italian King that afternoon.

'Who are you soldier,' he asked.

'Private Hans Job, IV Battalion, III Division, your Majesty,' said Heracles jumping to attention as the ground shock and wondering whether he had chosen a convincing name.

'Well Hans,' said Wilhelm, 'This is your lucky day. As head of the German Armed Forces I am immediately promoting you to the rank of Captain and assigning you to my Imperial Guard. What d'you say about that, eh ? No, don't bother thanking me. There isn't time. We're going to need to knock up a new uniform to fit you pretty damn quick for your first official duty this afternoon accompanying me when I greet the King of Italy. What d'you say about that, eh ?.'

'I'm honoured, your Majesty,' said Heracles, 'But I regret that I must decline your generous offer.'

'Whadda y'mean DECLINE MY OFFER ?,' spluttered the Kaiser, 'You can't decline my offer. Don't you realise the potential fame, wealth and glory you will get from becoming a member of my elite Imperial Guard.'

'I don't seek fame, wealth and glory, Majesty. Only to return to my peasant village in Alsace. You see sire, they need me. The farmers are so poor they can not afford a horse and they need me to pull the plough,' replied Heracles pathetically.

'You moron,' yelled Wilhelm, 'You could buy the sodding village with the money you'll be earning. Anyway, it doesn't matter whether you agree or not. You're a serving member of the German Armed Forces and if I order you to join my Imperial Guard, then that's what you do.'

'Not so, your Majesty,' insisted Heracles.

'I could have you shot for desertion,' screamed the Kaiser, his podgy face becoming scarlet and shaking with rage. 'Whadda y'mean NOT SO ?'

'Well Majesty,' continued Heracles, 'I've served seven years with my battalion. My papers have been filed with the proper authorities this morning and I'm due to be discharged from the army at noon today. In fact, I've got to catch a train from Berlin central station at 2 pm today to return to my village in Alsace. I was just killing a little time in the gymnasium during my last few hours in the army.'

Wilhelm slumped back onto a bench in shock as if he'd been struck by a giant club. Whilst he might have virtually absolute power over any member of the armed forces, in three hours time and one hour before the arrival of the Italian King, this man would be a civilian and on his way back home from the very spot where the little King Umberto would be stepping off his train. Even the German Kaiser couldn't legally compel a civilian who had completed his full military service back into the army against his will in time of peace. Wilhelm thought about having the law changed but realised he couldn't do this in a couple of hours. But it had now become an obsession. He was determined to have this seven foot giant among his Imperial Guard for his meeting with the Italian King.

From the day he'd been born Wilhelm had always got everything he ever wanted by screaming and bullying. This time though he realised this wasn't going to work and, unfamiliar though it was to him, in his desperation he decided he'd better try turning on a little charm.

'That's all right Hans,' he said, consolingly, 'Here m'lad, come and join me in this steam room. You still have a couple of hours to spare and I'd like to have a little chat with you alone. Just you and me. A couple of old soldiers together.'

Heracles felt a little uneasy about this, but followed the Kaiser into the steam room and sat down on a bench opposite him. To Heracles' relief

Wilhelm's mind seemed to be on other things.

'Now Hans,' he said, 'Forget all that stuff I just said about having you shot. I was only teasing. I quite understand if you want to get back to your village and don't want to join my Imperial Guard. It's all right, you don't have to.' Wilhelm patted Heracles on the lap reassuringly. 'But Hans, as a little favour to me, your emperor, couldn't you just delay your return for a few hours and help me out at a little function I'm attending this afternoon. As a favour to me; as a friend.'

'I could, your Majesty........,' started Heracles.

'Excellent,' quipped the Kaiser, clapping his hands together.

'......but I'm afraid I don't like you. Nobody back home likes you.'

'Huh,' spluttered Wilhelm. 'Whad y'mean ? Why doesn't anybody in Alsace like me ?'

'Because, Majesty,' replied Heracles, 'Ever since the province was liberated from the French thirty years ago they've never given up their cause of "la revanche"; their determination to once again enslave our sturdy German yeomen inside their contemptible republic. My countrymen are fearful that their farms are going to be overrun and their wives and daughters raped by savage French soldiers, and they blame you for that. They think its about time you took up the sword of Hermann and took care of the Latin menace for good.'

Wilhelm was shattered. He slumped back on the bench and came close to bursting out into tears. If there was one thought that an absolute ruler like himself could not bear to face it was the thought that he was anything other than universally loved by his people. After all everybody always told him he was; all the courtiers and palace officials, all the ministers and local dignitaries, all the army officers and all the servants; and yet here was this simple Alsatian peasant soldier letting him know; straight between the eyes, both barrels, no pussy footing around; that the common people hated him. Nightmare images flooded his head. He could see himself being ridiculed and reviled by crude craftsmen and labourers over their steins of ale in countless thousand beer halls across Germany, and he wished the ground would open up and swallow him.

Biting his trembling lower lip Wilhelm meekly asked, ' Wh...what can I do

?'

'There, there, Kaiser,' said Heracles, this time him patting Wilhelm's lap, 'Its not that bad. Your people would love you once again and their fears be allayed if you took the initiative and attacked France now.'

'But France has allied itself with Russia,' protested Wilhelm.

'All the more reason to hit them fast then,' Heracles reassured him, 'before Russia can come to France's aid.'

'What about the English though ?,' asked Wilhelm. 'If I move against France the English may threaten to blockade Germany by sea.'

'All the more reason then to get that great navy of yours moving and face England down. God knows we've had to swallow enough of their arrogance in the past. Now its time to stand up for the fatherland and their turn to stand down,' Heracles insisted.

'I see.' said Wilhelm.

'Kaiser,' said Heracles firmly, 'If you're the man I really think you are, one who will lead the German Empire to ever greater military glory, then I'm sure you will gain the universal affection of your people. And.......,' Heracles paused for dramatic effect, '..I suppose I could delay my return to Alsace for a few months and accept the honour of joining your Imperial Guard.'

Wilhelm's tear-stained face lit up like a child's. 'You'll do it,' he gasped in wonder, 'You'll be a part in my reception ceremony for the Italian King this afternoon ?'

'Yes Kaiser,' said Heracles. 'Provided you agree to do what I've suggested on the military front.'

'Oh Yes, Yes. Agreed. Agreed,' cried Wilhelm, 'Wunderbar, wunderbar.' And he jumped up a did a little jig around the steam room in his excitement.

'Now Hans,' said the Kaiser, calming down, 'We haven't any time to lose. You'll need to get over to the Imperial tailor straight away for him to be able to knock up a guardsman's uniform big enough to fit you in time for the ceremony. You get off now to get measured up, I'll send orders ahead, and I'll see you again this afternoon at the railway station.'

Heracles left. Wilhelm lay back on the bench and a huge smile of satisfaction broke out from ear to ear. 'Those fools in the Military High Command and the Foreign Office,' he thought to himself. 'Telling me I could trust the Russians and the English, taking seriously the French President's nonsense about wanting peace, and keeping our huge army tied up like a muzzled beast. And it takes a simple Alsatian soldier to point out the truth. Best of all, Hans will be in my entourage when I meet the Italian King this afternoon. Oooooh,' he said, 'rubbing his sweaty hands in glee, 'I just can't wait to see the dwarf's face when he steps off that train.'

The Kaiser got up and left the steam room to find the Foreign Minister, Von Holstein, and the chief of the general staff, Von Schlieffen, standing outside evidently having been waiting for some time to see him.

'What do you two dumpkoffs want ?' snapped Wilhelm. 'Von Schlieffen, I want you to get working on a plan to invade France right away.'

'Er.., certainly your Majesty,' replied the bemused General.

'Majesty,' said Von Holstein, 'You asked us for a report on the crisis in Italy. I'm afraid we've just received some very bad news.'

'Well ?,' demanded Wilhelm. 'More appeasement is it, more caution needed on our part I suppose, whatever it is.'

'Briefly sire,' continued Von Holstein, 'yesterday evening King Umberto of Italy was assassinated by socialist terrorists. The country is in chaos and it is questionable whether the new king, his son Victor Emmanuelle, will be able to restore order among the warring social and political factions. The situation is very serious.'

'Eh...?,' stuttered the Kaiser, not yet able to comprehend the words his ears were hearing. 'Does this mean the visits off then ?'

'Majesty,...Majesty ?' the Foreign Minister turned to the General, 'I think he's fainted.'

***

Chapter Five

Emperor Franz Josef, heir to the Holy Roman Emperors and the Hapsburg dynasty that had, at least nominally, ruled much of Europe over the preceding centuries tinkled the little bell on his breakfast table until his arthritic wrist ached, but still no one came. He couldn't understand where all his servants and nurses had gone. They'd wheeled him out onto the lawn in front of the sanatorium with its breathtaking vista of the snow-peaked Austrian Alps, tucked in his blanket, set up his breakfast table and now, it seems, totally disappeared. He tinkled the bell again as furiously he could until that provoked a bout of coughing, but still no one came.

His toast had been cut into the little strips he called his 'soldiers' and he was ready to dunk them into his boiled egg. But nobody had taken the top off the egg and it sat there on the plate next to the empty egg cup.

At 70 the Emperor's mind was getting a little slow and he couldn't remember whether he was meant to decapitate the egg at the blunt end or the pointy end. 'If they'd at least left it in the egg cup I would have known which end was the top, ' thought the old man, ' but lying on its side like that I can't tell.'

Franz knew he'd have to make a decision before the egg got too cold, but which end to take off ? Finally he resolved the dilemma by slicing off both ends. He then closed this eyes and twirled the egg on the plate, picking it up gingerly by the side and placing it in the egg cup so that he wouldn't see which way up it was going. Pleased with himself he triumphantly plunged one of his toast soldiers into the top of the egg, but unfortunately this only pushed all the material out through the bottom of the egg into a mess at the bottom of the egg cup.

'Look at me,' sobbed the Emperor to himself, 'In military college my classmates used to call me 'Swift & Deadly Franz' before the burden of running this empire robbed me of both my youth and my chance of proving myself on the field of valour. Now I can't even beat an egg.' The old man's head started to loll a little and his eyelids drop. 'Swift & Deadly......swift & deadly.......,' he was murmuring to himself

'Hey look, there goes Swift & Deadly Franz,' called a voice from the crowd.

'Cliff and Dudley who ?,' came a reply.

'No, no, Swift & Deadly Franz,' insisted the first voice. 'He's the nephew of the Emperor, the bravest and most dashing cavalry officer in the whole of the Austrian army. They're on their way to give the upstart King of Piedmont the thrashing he deserves.'

Prince Franz Josef von Hapsburg, commander of the corp cavalry brigade of the Austrian army, sat proudly erect astride his charger, leading his cavalrymen through the main streets of Trieste alongside the columns of Austrian foot soldiers and horse-drawn artillery carriages all marching west towards northern Italy where the King of Piedmont was challenging Austrian supremacy in the region. Franz cut a fine figure. His tall muscular frame emphasised by his smart cavalry uniform, the strong noble jaw and the fine, sharp sideburns that drove the young ladies of Vienna wild.

'What's happening to me,' thought Franz, 'I'm young and strong again. But I remember this. This isn't now, 1900. This is 1848. I'm eighteen again and on my way to what should have been my first great moment of military glory at the battle of Vicenza, stolen from me when my imbecile of an uncle abdicated and the throne passed to me.'

The Emperor looked up in shock He was back on the lawn of the sanatorium again. But he was no longer alone. Standing in front of the breakfast table stood a tall beautiful girl, her long brown hair flowing in the gentle breeze. She wore a short tunic exposing a pair of curvy legs tapering into leather sandals and across her shoulder she carried a large wooden bow and a quiver of arrows. Two large hunting dogs roamed around the lawn, one of them stopping next to the table and sniffing at Franz's messy egg cup.

Without saying a word the girl suddenly whipped round and in a split second loosed an arrow which went flying off into the field behind her. 'Fetch,' she called, and one of the dogs went bounding down the field in the direction of the now distant arrow to return minutes later with a hare between its jaws. The arrow shot clean though the hare's neck.

'Swift & Deadly' the girl said, enigmatically.

'Wh...Who are you,' Franz Josef asked meekly.

The girl didn't reply, instead she said, 'Would you like to visit the battle ?'

A tear rolled down the old man's face and he looked down at his trembling hands. He felt the aching in his limbs, the wheezing in his lungs and his uncomfortable bedsores. He would give anything, anything, to be young and strong again, and to experience that adrenaline-packed thrill that can only be found in the midst of a battlefield that he had always yearned for but been denied.

He looked up and a cannon ball screamed past him just six inches from his head to explode into a supply wagon behind him throwing Austrian soldiers and pieces of the wagon high into the air. The acrid smell of gunpowder filled his nose. All around was the chaos and the roar of battle; soldiers clashing here, horses charging there, artillery booming everywhere. Franz Josef was young again, no longer Emperor but a cavalry officer mounted on his charger and in the middle of the Battle of Vicenza, 1848.

He looked round and saw where the shot had come from. A group of Piedmontese infantry and artillery men were grouped around a cannon under a clump of trees, preparing to reload. Franz wheeled his stallion around, drew his sabre and charged at the group. 'Swift & Deadly!,' he yelled.

The soldiers loosed off a volley of musket shots. One whistled through Franz's left epaulette and another grazed his right arm as he charged towards them and they began to scatter in panic. But it was too late. He was upon them. The sabre rose gleaming in the sunlight, and fell, and rose again crimson, and fell again. In a frenzy Franz hacked at the unfortunate Italian soldiers until a full dozen off them lie with their life's blood oozing out onto the stained grass. The cannon had been primed and ready. Without pausing Franz dismounted his horse and grabbed at one of the canons wheels. His powerful body straining he slowly turned the huge artillery piece until it was pointing the other way, directly at the centre of the enemy front line where the final Austrian push was just beginning to falter. The grapeshot ripped through the Piedmontese scattering their defensive lines. At this signal the Austrian troops, who had been steadily falling back, took heart and charged the breech in the enemy centre. The Piedmontese lines first buckled, then broke and then it turned into a rout.

With the sound of 'Hurrah for Swift & Deadly Franz, hero of the battle of Vicenza,' dying in his ears the old man looked up at the beautiful young girl standing before him.

'How can I ever thank you,' he said, 'I never thought I would ever have the chance to know such ecstasy.'

'War is such a noble occupation,' said the girl. 'So clean, so honest, so glorious.'

'Yes,' agreed the Emperor.

'If you want me to take you to more battlefields you must first create them,' she said. 'The once great Hapsburg Empire is in decline. As the Slavs, the Bulgars and a host of other races break away from the dying Ottoman Empire and assert their claims to independent nationhood they threaten to incite similar nationalist sentiment and insurrection amongst the subject races of your empire. You know what you must do.'

And somehow Franz did know with crystal clarity. How dare the French and the English challenge his ancient and divine right to rule over the people of the Balkans. And the Kaiser and the Tsar. Did they really think that the mighty Austro-Hungarian Empire had gone soft just because its Emperor had aged a little bit. Well Franz would show them. He wasn't that old yet and there was still time for even greater glory to be won.

'I will come to you again,' said the girl. And with that she and the dogs were gone.

Franz Josef closed his eyes for a moment and again savoured the thrill of the battlefield. 'Oh your Majesty, look what a mess you've made of your egg. Shall I get you another one so you can dunk your soldiers in it properly. I said shall I get you another egg ?' said the voice of the Emperor's butler.

But it wasn't egg Franz was planning to dunk his soldiers in anymore. 'Where the hell have you been, leaving me alone out here all this time ?,' he cursed at the butler.

'But Majesty,' insisted the butler, startled by the normally docile old man's uncharacteristic vigour, 'I've only been gone an instant to get your warm milk. Are you feeling all right ?'

'Never felt better,' replied the Emperor. 'And get cook to fix that up for my dinner,' he said, gesturing at the dead hare that lay on the ground by the side of the breakfast table.

* * *

Chapter Six

Robert Arthur Talbot Gascoyne-Cecil, Third Marquess of Salisbury and Prime Minister of Great Britain and Ireland nervously paced the gardens of his family estate, Hatfield House. He was shortly due an important visitor. A most important visitor. This assignation had been arranged through intermediaries only the previous day under conditions of the utmost secrecy, but such was the importance of the individual concerned and the potential gravity of the issue to be discussed to the very fabric and future of the British Empire; an Empire spanning one quarter of the globe and on which the sun never set; that even the Prime Minister was obliged to drop every thing else for this meeting. He had even had to cancel a ride with the hunt planned for that day.

Salisbury might have noticed the unusually lavish fecundity of his gardens that summer morning, but his mind was on other things. He was terrified at what he might be about to hear and, as a result, whether or not there might still be a British Empire in a few months time.

He heard the horse carriage pull up in the courtyard on the other side of the building and the sound of his butler greeting his visitor. A minute or so later the butler came out to let him know the visitor was ready to see him in his sitting room. Salisbury took a deep breath, clenched his fists, and entered the house.

'Your Royal Highness, always such a great honour and a great pleasure to see you,' intoned the Prime Minister as he entered the sitting room.

'Cut the crap Robert. He's been at it again and you know it.' she spat back at him.

Sitting in his favourite armchair, eyes blazing with fury, was Princess Alexandra, the wife of Prince Albert, Prince of Wales. The imminent King of Great Britain and Emperor of India.

'Your Highness,' drooled Salisbury, 'I assure you all that business with the actress Lilly Langtree ended long ago. Prince Louis of Battenberg, the First Sea Lord, is shafting her now.'

'Its not her anymore Robert,' insisted the Princess, 'Its all those French whores. Him and his bloody "entente cordiale". Why do you think he keeps going backwards and forwards to Paris every five minutes. That French President with his phoney alliance plans is not the only one Bertie goes sucking up to when he's over there. You know what these French women are like Robert. You may sit down.'

'Thank you,' the Prime Minister sat. 'Your Highness,' Salisbury said in his most pompous politician's voice, 'His Majesty's Government places the utmost importance on the maintenance and preservation of our alliance with France. Your husband, ma'am, in his special relationships with France, has been of immeasurable assistance to our efforts in this respect.'

'Right then,' snapped back the Princess. 'If you won't do anything about it I want a divorce.'

'A w-w-w-what ?,' spluttered Salisbury, fearing he might be having a heart attack.

'A D...I...V...O...R...C...E. Christ, have I got to sing it !'

'But Your Highness,' begged Salisbury, 'You're the future Queen of England, you're married to the future King, the head of the British Empire. You can't get a divorce.'

The Princess stood her ground. 'We'll see about that. I reckon, king or not, if he's going to keep going over to France and shafting everything that moves, then I can get a divorce.'

'Please Your Highness,' Salisbury was becoming frantic. 'The Monarchy is the cement that holds the entire British Establishment together. Without the Royal Family what would we become. We would descend into coarseness and vulgarity, governments would succumb to the wishes of the masses, and the common people would lose respect for their betters. A divorce between the future King and Queen of England would destroy the monarchy and that would destroy Britain itself.'

'So what are you going to do to stop him keep going over to France,' demanded Alexandra.

'What can I do Your Highness ? He's the future King. How can I stop him travelling backwards and forwards to France if he insists ?' Salisbury thought that was a rhetorical question. He was wrong.

'You could declare war on France,' she said. 'Then there wouldn't be any travel between England and France and Bertie would have to stay at home where I can keep an eye on him.'

'But Your Highness,' pleaded Salisbury, 'An alliance with France is our only hope of countering the growing threat of Germany. Meanwhile we're up to our necks in this wretched war in South Africa.'

Princess Alexandra looked at him sternly, 'Piss or get off the pot Robert. Which do you, as Prime Minister, think is the bigger threat to the future of the British Empire.'

Salisbury was beaten. 'You win Your Highness. I'll advise your mother-in-law tomorrow that her government will be declaring war on France,' he said solemnly.

'Good boy,' said Hera.

* * *

Chapter Seven

Apollo stood on a hill and surveyed the parched Turkish landscape around him. To his west he could see the coast and the blue waters of the Adriatic Sea stretching out towards his home in Mount Olympus but it was the small huddle of huts, tents, caravans and activity taking place admidst the otherwise desolate scene to his east that held his fascination and for which he had made this special pilgrimage on his way to find the Sultan in Constantinople.

There below him they were uncovering the very walls that he and Poseidon had been forced by Zeus to build as a punishment for their taking part in an earlier revolt. Those walls that had stood at the beginning of western history but had finally been destroyed by the Greeks some three millennia ago and had since lain buried and forgotten by mankind until they were rediscovered only a few years earlier.

Of all the affairs of man none had ever had such an impact nor made such a lasting impression on the gods of Olympus as the Trojan War. It was the zenith of their age. An age of heroes and exploits. An age of excellence, when mortals would appeal for the favour of their patron divinity with due ceremony and respect, and the gods were free to answer those calls.

The war had been caused in the first place by the enmity aroused between Hera, Athena and Aphrodite after the goddess of love had bribed Paris, a prince of Troy, into selecting her as the fairest of the three with the award of a golden apple. Paris' prize was the abduction of the beautiful Helen, wife of a Greek King Menelaus, which in turn led to the Greek invasion of Troy and ten long years of siege before the stalemate was finally broken when the Greeks tricked their way into the city by hiding inside a huge wooden horse.

Even now, thousands of years later, Hera and Athena had never forgiven Aphrodite and once again this feud threatened to unleash a terrible war on mankind. But now a truly terrible war. Not at all like the Trojan War where mighty heroes like Achilles and Hector had fought in mortal combat in front of the gates of Troy watched and cheered on by their respective armies; the Trojans lining the walls of the city and the Greeks from their siege lines. That was warfare fought between giants among men who knew precisely what they were fighting for; honour and excellence. Nothing like the coming maelstrom where faceless common men would slaughter each other from a distance in their millions and none of them would even know what it was they were dying for.

Apollo looked up and to his north in the glimmering haze he could make out the ancient Hellespont; now called the Dardanelles; the vital strategic waterway that separated Europe from Asia. He remembered how, some six hundred years after the fall of Troy the Persian King Darius had built a bridge of boats to transport his massive invasion force across the water on their way to defeat at the hands of the Greeks. But even by then these were a new type of Greeks. Greeks to whom the heroes of the Trojan War were no more than legend and the stuff of stories. Greeks who were already turning their backs on the gods and the old values of honour, beauty and excellence and instead putting their faith in the power of supposedly clever argument and flawed absolute truths. In the two and a half millennia since, as the gods had watched passively, forbidden by Zeus to intervene after the fractures of the Trojan War, man had continued to grow ever more clever with himself as he had grown ever more shameful.

Apollo stood watching the archaeological site, wreathed in glorious memories of a past that would never come again, occasionally catching the sound drifting up from the camp of some order barked in German. Slowly the setting sun illuminated the Adriatic in crimson and gold. A tear rolled down the god's cheek as the sky began to darken and the air grew colder. He finally turned his back and headed north for the city of Constantinople.

* * *

For one thousand years after the collapse of the Roman Empire in the west the Byzantine Emperors had kept alive the traditions and the guise of the old Empire in the east from the city of Constantinople. Through the long dark and medieval ages, whilst a much ravaged Rome had fallen into decay and Athens had become little more than a memory, the city on the Bosphorus straddling two continents which Constantine the Great, the first Christian Emperor, had made his capital stood like a beacon of civilisation and culture; a city large enough itself to contain the populations of every western capital.

Finally, after withstanding countless sieges and having held back from Europe the storm of Islam for centuries, the city was bought down, not by Muslim hordes, but by fellow Christians meant to be passing through on their way to liberate the Holy Land from the infidel who had instead decided they had more to gain by plundering the unimaginable wealth they saw all around them in their host city. The Eastern Empire never fully recovered from this calamity and in 1453 finally fell to the Ottoman Turk Mehmet the Conqueror. Within a hundred years the Turks had overrun the entire Balkans and Vienna itself was under siege. This conquest also cut Europe off from its precious supply of spices from the far east and led directly to Columbus setting sail in search of another route for this vital commodity and accidentally discovering a New World along the way.

Still overcome with nostalgia Apollo surveyed the ruins of the ancient Hippodrome. This had once been the centre of Byzantine society, its marbled seats providing for 100,000 spectators who thronged to watch and gamble on the furious chariot races and other public entertainments, now barely recognisable but for the outline of its race track surrounding an Egyptian obelisk and some ruined columns. The whole length of the ancient circus was now overshadowed by the huge dome and six minarets of the Blue Mosque and to its north workmen were busily putting the finishing touches to a garish helmet-shaped fountain, a gift from the Kaiser to the people of Constantinople to mark his forthcoming visit.

Further to the north, beyond the great dome of the ancient cathedral of St. Sophia, itself now made a mosque with the crude addition of two stone minarets, Apollo passed by the Topkapi Palace, the sprawling home of the Ottoman Sultans, built originally by Mehmet after his conquest of the city, its harems, libraries, baths, council chambers, barracks, schools, kitchens, mosques, mints, fountains and gardens gradually added to by succeeding Sultans until it had become a city within a city. Only some fifty years earlier had the Sultan Abdul Mecit moved the royal residence to the more modern and westernised Dolmabachce Palace to the north of the Golden Horn on the west bank of the Bosphorus before drinking himself to death there but his grandson, the present Sultan Abdul Hamid II, had preferred to construct and live in his own version of Topkapi, the labyrinthine Yildiz Palace. It was here that Apollo was heading.

Hundreds of architects, builders and craftsmen had laboured to construct the Yildiz Palace but not one of them knew more than only a little part of the whole scheme. Behind its high fortified walls lay a maze of buildings, underground tunnels and secret passages linking the various residences, the harem, a private menagerie, guard posts, offices and countless storerooms where fabulous treasures accumulated by the Ottoman Sultans over centuries lie alongside worthless junk and files stacked to the ceilings full of reports from the army of spies, agent provocateurs and secret policemen employed throughout the crumbling empire.

In the deepest and darkest recess of this bizarre complex; more the reflection of a disturbed state of mind than a palace; sat the Old Spider himself, Sultan Abdul Hamid II, his nervous eyes regularly darting up underneath his fez to search the empty room for some unseen threat before returning to pour over his reports of sedition, secession, mutiny and rebellion, real and imagined, from his countless spies.

Abdul Hamid had been disliked by his father who suspected the boy of being an illegitimate child of an Armenian. His mother had been made a virtual outcast in the harem and had died when the awkward and withdrawn child was just seven years old. After his father was deposed in 1876 his older brother Murad had become Sultan but his reign ended after just three months when it became apparent that Murad was stark raving mad. It was then that the hitherto little known Abdul ascended as the heir of Mehmet the Conqueror and Suleiman the Magnificent, but Abdul Hamid II was neither a conqueror nor magnificent. He was though every bit as mad as his brother, but Abdul's madness was different. He kept it inside.

In fact, he kept himself inside. Never leaving the confines of his Yildiz sanctuary but for a brief visit every Friday to attend the Selamlik at a small mosque specially built just outside the palace for the purpose. Even inside, at the very centre of the tortured web that he alone knew the full design of, Abdul Hamid lived in constant terror that some assassins bullet or poisoners' brew would take his life. So great was his neurosis that he even refused to eat his meals off plates demanding instead that he dine from the cupped hands of his concubines.

Outside the Yildiz was a world full of enemies, both at home and abroad.

From the Great Powers who had arrogantly parcelled out Ottoman territory in the Balkans at the Congress of Berlin but who craved yet still more. From the Christian and countless ethnic minorities throughout his Empire all clambering for ever more autonomy and independence. From the liberal-minded reformers of the Young Turk movement at home and in exile abroad all demanding western style constitutional reform and an end to his absolute despotism. Above all the hated Armenians. At least he'd been able to atone for the insults of his youth by ordering the massacre of some tens of thousands of their men, women and children in eastern Anatolia at the hands of barbaric Kurdish tribesmen a few years earlier. An act that had earned for him the opprobrium of the civilised world.

As his enemies and their hatred of him multiplied so Abdul Hamid sank ever deeper into the recesses of the Yildiz and the recesses of his own manic insecurity, trusting nobody or nothing but the reports of his secret agents and the forecasts of his astrologers.

A little bell tinkled above the voice tube fixed to the wall. Nobody but Abdul alone was ever allowed to enter his inner office and his servants were obliged to contact him and take their instructions through a long rubber pipe linking the room to the outside world. The Sultan gingerly lifted the ear and mouth piece, checking as he always did lest some poison had been smeared around its edges, and when he was satisfied he sighed down the tube, 'Yes ?'

'Your Majesty,' came the voice of his valet whistling down the tube, 'you asked me to let you know when the new astrologer arrived. He's now waiting in the audience chamber at your pleasure.'

'Have all the guards been posted and this astrologer thoroughly checked for any concealed weapons or suchlike ?,' asked the Sultan.

'Yes, Your Majesty, of course,' said the aide.

'Fine. Never hurts to be too careful. I'll be along shortly,' he said.

* * *

After the indignities of his search, which had involved removing his silken robes and turban and having his every last orifice examined by the palace eunuchs, Apollo was now starting to become a little irritated lying prostrate face down on the floor, his arms outstretched, waiting on this mortal even if he was the Sultan. Finally, just as his patience was beginning to snap and he was thinking about calling the whole thing off, he heard the Sultan enter, ascend his throne and, after a brief pause and buzz of huddled conversation the order, 'You may rise.'

Apollo stood up in the large audience chamber. Sumptuous Turkish carpets covered the floor and walls and the ceilings were adorned with brightly coloured tiles. In front of him the Sultan sat on a raised throne in a radiant halo of sunlight pouring in through a stained-glass window behind him. Beneath the Sultan's red fez two beady little eyes peered anxiously at him through a carpet of bushy grey eyebrows, beard and moustache mounted atop a tunic so bedecked with golden epaulettes, sashes, medals and braid that Apollo wondered how he managed to stand. The Sultan gestured towards a small table containing cups of what Apollo realised would be the foul tasting coffee so beloved by the Turks.

'Thank you, Your Majesty,' he said, and he quickly drained a small cup of the thick liquid trying not to wince.

'They tell me you can foretell the future,' said Abdul at length.

'Majesty,' replied Apollo, 'I am but a humble seeker after the truth but if Allah in his wisdom has blessed me with the special gift of insight into his grand design as written in the heavens then I in turn can only put this gift in the service of his Caliph.'

'Then what do you see for the future of my Empire ?,' asked the Sultan.

'I see Taurus the Bull. I see the Great Bear. I see Aquilla the Eagle. And I see the crescent moon,' replied Apollo, making a great show of consulting his charts. 'The bull is lost in the dark, looking for the light of the moon to guide it to safety, but the crescent moon is dim and the bull cannot find its way. In the darkness both the bear and the eagle wait to lure the bull into a trap. Then, just as the bull is about to fall prey to the claws of the bear and the talons of the eagle, a bright light rises in the east. It is Orion the mighty hunter. He takes the bull and leads it safely towards the light of the moon. The moon then grows more powerful until it blazes like a thousand suns and the terrified bear and eagle flee before it.'

Abdul Hamid was now sitting forward on the edge of his throne, totally captivated and hanging on every word. 'What does this all mean ?,' he asked in wonder.

'Majesty,' replied Apollo. 'The bull is the country of Bulgaria, led astray from the light of the Turkish Empire, the crescent moon, by the bear, Russia, and the eagle, the Austrians. The light of our Empire grows dim and we cannot guide our subject people onto the true path of loyalty and obedience and away from the predators that wait to ensnare them.'

'I see, I see,' enthused the Sultan. 'But what of Orion. He leads the bull to safety, doesn't he? And the moon grows strong again and routs the bear and the eagle.'

'Majesty,' cried out Apollo, dropping down on one knee and stretching out his arms for dramatic effect. 'You are Orion. You are that mighty hunter who will lead Bulgaria back to the safety of your embrace, restore the Ottoman Empire to its former magnificence and send the Russian and Austrian infidels fleeing before you.'

'Allah be praised,' cried the Sultan. 'I always knew it. I always knew I was his chosen one. I just needed a sign. Oh thank you, thank you.'

'Even now, Your Majesty,' said Apollo solemnly, 'the spies and the rabble rousers of the Emperor and the Tsar are operating in Bulgaria hoping to complete the process begun twenty years ago of formally tearing the country away. Once Bulgaria is gone nothing will prevent the total break up of the Empire. Macedonia, Palestine, Arabia, Armenia will all be next. Only your resolute action now can turn the tide. No more vacillation. No more giving way to the demands of the western powers or treacherous local demagogues. You must march your army into Bulgaria and reassert Ottoman authority over the country and its people as the first step in expelling the Austrians and the Russians from the whole of the Balkans. Your strength and resolve will re-unite behind you and re-empower the whole of the Turkish people and the western world will once again tremble before the might of the Ottoman Empire.'

'I'll do it,' cried the enraptured Sultan. 'In the name of Allah I swear I'll do it.'

'That's the spirit,' beamed Apollo. To himself he said, 'Well, I think I've done my job pretty well. He can't get into too much trouble sodding about at the back end of nowhere in this wretched Bulgaria place. This palace gives me the creeps but I guess I'd better just check out his harem before I take off for good.'

* * *

Apollo had only three real interests in life. Wine, women and song. His stock advice to mortals on the subject was, 'When you get too old for wine, women and song, then give up singing.'

After a quick roll call of the Sultan's harem he decided he'd had enough of Turkey and thought he might as well look in on Aphrodite in France and see what was going on between her and this Loubet character. On his way across the Brenner Pass heading west he bumped into Hermes going the other way.

'Hi ya Stud,' called Hermes cheerfully. 'What are you doing here. I thought you were supposed to be in Turkey stopping the Sultan from conquering the world ?'

'That's none of your business, delivery boy,' snapped back Apollo.

'Suit yourself,' said Hermes, 'But I don't have to tell Zeus I saw you here. He can get pretty upset when his orders are disobeyed.'

Apollo thought better of it. 'Hey, little buddy, stay loose,' he said, 'You don't have to tell the boss man everything, you know. Say, how's about you'n me sit down by those rocks over there and try a little of this Turkish Delight I picked up in the Sultan's harem.'

Apollo and Hermes sat down on a clump of warm rocks as the bright summer sunshine illuminated the splendid alpine panorama stretched out beneath them. They started on the Turkish Delight.

'So, what have the other gods been getting up to with their men ?,' Apollo asked Hermes.

A little later the two of them were rolling around the rocks in fits of uncontrollable giggles. 'Tell me again about Heracles and the Kaiser in the steam room,' spluttered Apollo, crouched on the rocks grabbing his chest as his sides split with laughter and the tears rolled down his face. 'Or Aphrodite with that floppy Frenchman,' roared Hermes, nearly falling over the ledge in his mirth.

This persisted for some time.

Eventually as the shadows started to pass across the mountains the two began to calm down and fell very mellow.

'Well I guess I better be one my way,' said Hermes finally. ' I think I may look in on Turkey.'

'So what's the score with Zeus anyway,' Apollo asked. 'Isn't he going to be upset if all the gods are making such a dogs breakfast of his instructions to stop the European nations all rushing into war with each other ?'

'Oh,' said Hermes, 'I think he'll learn to live with it.'

* * *

Chapter Eight

After completing his survey of the activities of the gods with their individual clients it was late March before Hermes returned to Mount Olympus to report his findings to Zeus. He found the king of the gods in his lounge studying the pool intently.

'Howdy boss,' he beamed, 'Anything much happening at the moment down there.'

'I'm not sure I like what I'm seeing, but you better let me have your report first,' said Zeus.

'But boss,' said Hermes, 'its going like a dream. Those mortal fools are all primed and ready to explode into war with each other. You were absolutely right when you said all the other gods would ignore your instructions to try and calm down the situation. Instead they've all provoked their chosen man into actually going to war. I don't think anything can go wrong now.'

'Hmmm,' said Zeus. 'Well, what have they been up to ?'

'Well,' said Hermes consulting a notebook he had lifted from one of his winged boots, this being the only place he had to keep such items other than under his winged helmet. 'Le'me see, Aphrodite first.'

'She played the Frenchman like a violin, boss, brilliant. President Loubet has amassed huge wealth and power in France but none of that can give him the one thing he really wants in life. Aphrodite is the only woman who can give him that and he's hopelessly in love with her. He's got her holed up in an apartment in a classy part of Paris where he visits her three times a week to receive his instructions.'

'French public opinion is still smarting over their humiliation last year when France and England came to the brink of war about whose flag should be flown over a dilapidated fort in the African desert. The French had to climb down at the time and Loubet has had little difficulty in persuading his government that this affront to French dignity needs to be avenged.'

'Even as we speak, special teams of French engineers are working in conditions of the utmost secrecy to complete a tunnel under the English Channel which is nearly ready. This will allow the French army to suddenly appear in Kent, bypassing the Royal Navy that has always protected England from invasion, from where they should be able to quickly march on London and overwhelm the much smaller British land forces. Its not a bad plan, boss.'

'Can they build such a tunnel in time ?,' asked Zeus.

'They seem to think so,' Hermes replied. 'They recently built a very successful canal linking the Mediterranean with the Red Sea which, to the further annoyance of the French, the English have since seized control of. Recovering the Suez Canal and expelling the English from Egypt is the first item on the list of demands that the French expect to dictate at the eventual peace treaty. They only have to use the tunnel once, so they don't have to build it to last and it need be no wider than is necessary to drive a horse and carriage or march a column of soldiers through in one direction. Their High Command are already working on complex schedules that will allow them to begin loading the tunnel the preceding night and from dawn start pouring 10,000 soldiers an hour, complete with cavalry and artillery, into the English countryside just sixty miles south east of London. Within 24 hours they reckon they can put through enough French soldiers to outnumber the entire British army, which they think will be dispersed around the country and in Ireland with no time to organise themselves.'

'And where will the British army actually be ?,' asked Zeus.

'You should have seen Hera boss. You'd be proud of your wife, it was a star performance. She disguised herself as the future Queen of England and is blackmailing the English Prime Minister into going to war with France otherwise she'll cause a scandal that will rock the foundations of the British Empire. The English establishment are so obsessed with their monarchy that its been easier for them to persuade themselves that they have a genuine grievance over French incursions into the southern Sahara and therefore, conveniently, it seems that they are at one with the Princess' wishes. For good measure Hera also well and truly wrecked the plans of the English Prince of Wales who's been playing a crucial role recently in rebuilding relations between Britain and France.'

'English war preparations are well under way. They plan to surprise the French in the Spring with a night time dash across the channel and dawn landings at a place called Dieppe on the northern French coast 100 miles north of the French capital. From there they will then quickly drive on Paris before the French government or the French army, which they think will be deployed 200 miles to the east along their border with Germany, realise what's happening. They expect that by nightfall they'll be holding Paris, which the French won't dare to attack, and that the largely hostage French government will have no choice but to agree to their peace terms, which will include ceding to Britain France's colonies and domination in Africa.'

'What about Germany,' said Zeus.

'Well the Kaiser has become totally infatuated with Heracles, who is now Captain of his Imperial Guard and his closest personal advisor. Heracles has shamed him over his many recent blunders and diplomatic climb downs and convinced Kaiser Bill that only firm action will restore respect for him. The German public are baying for war over any and every little incident anyway, it has been over thirty years since they last had one after all, which is a long time for them, and the High Command are straining at the lease to attack France in the Spring with what they call their plans for a 'lightning war'. This involves the German army bypassing the French, who they also think will be dug in along their borders to the south-east, by attacking through the neutral country of Belgium, sweeping down along the poorly defended channel coast, and encircling Paris from the north and west.'

'So all three armies will be marching at about the same time in roughly the same part of the world.' noted Zeus.

'Precisely the same time,' replied Hermes. 'Spurred on by their respective divinities, the leaders of France, Britain and Germany have all secretly pencilled in 1st April 1901 as the date when they plan to launch their respective invasions. It should be hilarious. Whilst the British army cross the English Channel to invade France, unbeknownst to them the French army will be travelling through their tunnel going the other way a thousand feet underneath their ships. The French army should pop up in England just as their own country is invaded by Germany whose forces will be storming down the channel coast to run into, not the French army, but the British. The confusion should be indescribable.'

What about the other three powers ?' asked Zeus.

'Well they should all clash headlong into each other on, let me see,' Hermes said with a smile, pretending to consult his notebook, '1st of April.'

'How did I guess,' said Zeus.

'Ares certainly knew what he was doing when he choose the Balkans to start stirring things up between the powers boss,' said Hermes. 'The whole area is one big tinderbox waiting to blow. The region is technically part of the Ottoman Empire but for the past few decades Austria and Russia have both been sponsoring rebellions and the establishment of little independent client kingdoms at the expense of the Turks. The focus of attention now is a country called Bulgaria which is poised to throw off the last vestiges of Ottoman suzerainty and both Austria and Russia are determined to bring the new kingdom into their own camp.'

'Artemis comes to the senile old ruler of the Habsburg Empire bewitching his mind with visions of military glory which have spurred him into ordering a new Balkan adventure. At this very moment units of the the Austrian army are slipping quietly into the territory of its ally Serbia, ready to cross the border, re-establish order in the revolting Bulgaria and annex it as a part of their empire. At the same time they plan to annex the nominally Ottoman territory of Bosnia-Herzegovina which they are already occupying anyway and, since this move will inflame the Serbians who have been hoping for Bosnia themselves, and their forces will already be occupying Serbia with the Serbs' own agreement, they're going to annex Serbia as well, ruthlessly crushing any internal opposition. Thus at a stroke the Austrian Empire plans to grab most of the Balkans and, they think, without hardly needing to fire a shot or face any serious military opposition.'

'But ?,' said Zeus.

'But,' said Hermes, 'on the same day the Russian army, having taken up position along the borders with Bulgaria in the territory of their Rumanian ally, will move in and wrest the kingdom from the Turks as the first stage of a war with the Ottoman Empire that will put Russia in control of Constantinople, the Dardanelles and the Black Sea, and give Russia its long cherished warm water access to the Mediterranean.'

'Tsar Nicholas is absolute ruler of Russia. He can order this on his nation without fear of dissent and presently he's receiving his orders from Athena who visits the morose and withdrawn Tsar as the ghost of his dead mother. What they don't realise is that the Tsar's armies, when they move into Bulgaria from the east, will run slap bang into the Austrian Emperor's forces moving in from the west.'

'And what of the Sultan,' asked Zeus.

'Well it seems that, not without some encouragement from Apollo, Abdul Hamid II, Sultan of the Ottoman Empire, has decided that enough is enough. For decades little pieces of his empire in the Balkans have been fragmenting off and the remainder is in constant rebellion and turmoil. Abdul Hamid has now resolved to reassert Turkish authority in the region by marching his army into Bulgaria in the Spring and crushing all internal dissent to his rule.'

Zeus sat for some time reflecting on what Hermes had just told him.

'So there you have it boss,' Hermes said, starting to get a little impatient. 'Its perfect. Exactly as you imagined. Each of the leaders of the six Great Powers thinks that he alone is planning a surprise military adventure in the Spring that will give him glory and advance his nation's territorial ambitions. Each thinks that they can pull off their respective plans quickly and at little military cost since in every case they expect to be able to surprise the enemy in poorly defended areas with overwhelming force. Sure, they then expect a lot of huffing and puffing from the other powers followed by some international peace conference so everyone can get their snouts into the trough, as is their standard practise whenever these "crises" have blown up in the past, but they each reckon that by that time they'll be holding enough cards to be able to consolidate their gains.'

'Of course, what in practise will happen is that they will all run slap bang into each other, all tooled up for a war which none of them really wants or could even comprehend, and with the hardware, armies and navies they've now got facing each other this is going to make the Trojan War look like an argument at a dance.'

Hermes watched Zeus as he continued to scowl silently at the pool, twisting at his beard in that annoying habit of his.

'What's up boss, I thought you'd be pleased,' he eventually asked.

'I dunno,' said Zeus finally, 'I'm not sure I like it. I'm not sure I want it all to go ahead.'

'Whhhatt...,' said Hermes. 'Its a little late for that isn't it. Why not. Don't tell me you've suddenly become worried about all those millions of mortals who are going to die.'

'Of course not,' said Zeus.

'Well what then,' demanded Hermes.

Lightning flashed and a deep roar shock the ground as the king of the gods angrily rounded on his messenger who fell back in fright, realising he had gone too far. 'Don't talk to me like that,' Zeus thundered, 'That's the problem. Everybody around here seems to think that what I say doesn't matter anymore. That they can ignore my instructions and do what they like. Just because I've been asleep for a hundred years. Well I think its high time that I started showing people who's boss around here again. And we can start with a little less flippancy from you. Why didn't you tell me anything about Apollo leaving Turkey and travelling to France.'

'Er, I'm sorry boss,' pleaded Hermes, 'I was going to. I promise. I just never got that far.' Whatever foolish rebellion Ares and Poseidon were staging, Hermes knew full well that no other god or goddess could afford to lose their temper with or risk trying to curb the will of Zeus.

Zeus began to calm down a little. Hermes was still very useful to him and if he was going to have something of a fight on his hands in order to restore his authority then he might as well keep his able messenger on board; at least for the time being.

'So what would you like to do now boss ?,' ventured Hermes. 'As ever, as your trusted servant I await your bidding.'

'That's a bit more like it,' said Zeus. 'Well, I'm not sure. I suppose the first thing is to deal with Ares and Poseidon. For the moment the other gods have only ignored my instructions to keep their respective leaders from going to war, but those two are the ones that started the whole thing and they are openly challenging my supremacy.'

'What about the mortals and their plans to go to war in the Spring ?,' asked Hermes.

'Well I don't care about them,' said Zeus, 'but I'm buggered if I'm going to let those two bloodthirsty traitors enjoy the fruits of their efforts by seeing millions of mortals massacre each other on battlefields across Europe. How soon do you think it would take to get the various gods to call off their men ?'

'Tricky, boss,' confided Hermes. 'As you rightly guessed, each of the gods have started to identify the fortunes of their own reputation with the military success of their chosen puppet leader. They're all now pretty bloodthirsty themselves for the coming adventures which they've engineered and they're all taking a pride in their own handiwork. I can't see any of them easily giving this up now. Maybe they won't go as far as outright rebellion, maybe just prevarication and foot dragging, but with Ares and Poseidon still on the loose and flaunting your authority, do you really want to risk all out confrontation. Anyway, the invasions are all planned to take place within the next few days. Its probably too late to stop it.'

'No, you're right,' said Zeus. 'We'd better deal conclusively with Ares and Poseidon first. What news of them ?'

'I didn't get to see either of them I'm afraid boss,' said Hermes, 'but I know where Poseidon's hiding. He's presently holed up in an old disused smugglers cave on the Isle of Wight off the southern coast of England. From there he reckons he'll have a perfect vantage point to watch the English, French and Germans invade each other.'

'And Ares ?'

'Gone to ground I'm afraid boss,' said Hermes. 'I did manage to trace him and he's been real busy, but I'm afraid the scent went cold about nine months ago when all this started.'

'What's he been doing then ?,' asked Zeus.

'Well,' continued Hermes. 'For several years he was masquerading as a Greek arms dealer under the name of Boris Zararoff. In addition to doing everything he could to make sure that all the great powers got as tooled up as they possibly could; always encouraging one to buy ever more to keep up with what he had just sold to another; Ares' plans have been even more ambitious. He's not content with only starting a global war. Once its started he wants to keep it going for years, forcing the nations of Europe to plunge ever more of their millions of people into the carnage. To this end he has for many years been stockpiling phenomenal quantities of explosives and ammunitions in a secret location ready to feed these to the arms hungry nations of Europe once war has started, and to go on feeding them year after year until the entire continent is in ruins.'

'He's a nasty piece of work,' said Zeus. 'Is there no chance of you finding him and where he's got this stockpile ?'

'I'll find him eventually,' said Hermes, 'but it could take some time as he's been covering his tracks carefully. Anyway the wars are due to start any moment now.'

'Right, 'said Zeus firmly, 'here's what we'll do. I think its about time I paid Poseidon a little visit myself since we at least know where he is. Since he's off the coast of England I may as well look in on my errant wife and call time on her little game while I'm at it.'

'What do you want me to do boss ?,' asked Hermes.

'Well, see what you can do to stop the rest of them going to war. Visit the other gods and warn them that they risk incurring my wrath unless they get their men to call off the wars. And see if you can get any more information on Ares whereabouts. As soon as I've finished with Poseidon I'm going to have to deal with him,' replied Zeus.

'That's a pretty tall order,' protested Hermes. 'The planned invasions are all about to be launched. I'll never get round to all five of the others in time, let alone run down where Ares is hiding.'

'Well do what you can,' said Zeus. 'Are you still here, you'd better get a move on if its that tough an assignment.'

***

Chapter Nine

The young man resembled any other Parisian artist from the Latin Quarter with his long coat flapping in the early morning breeze, his easel, brushes and paint box tucked under one arm. He picked his way past the milk carts and urchins playing in the street along the Rue des Nonnains, across the Pont Marie and onto the tiny Isle St Louis, turning down its narrow cobbled Rue Saint-Louis lined with small cafes and the entrances to the upstairs apartment blocks.

The shops and cafes were all still closed and all was quiet on this bright March morning in the city of love. A few old concierges scrubbed at their doorsteps and a cafe owner in his vest hosed the debris from the night before out into the central gutter of the street where a pair of dogs began to tussle over the remains of a discarded chicken leg.

The young artist finally stopped outside an apartment block, placed his materials carefully on the ground and gave a smart rap on the front door. After a wait of some time he detected a stirring from an apartment above. Finally an old wooden shutter was flung upon and a figure appeared at the window. He looked up in anticipation and then dived back out of the way as a hand appeared and flung the contents of a chamber pot splashing onto the cobbles at his feet.

The head of a blousy Mademoiselle, her hair wrapped in a scarf and with a cigarette dangling from her lips, appeared at the window. Her drooping eyelids and smeared makeup clearly attesting to a night of bohemian excess in the pleasure capital of Europe. The young man looked up at her. It might have been a scene that was being replayed all over Paris that, and every, morning.

'Whadda you want ?,' she said.

'To paint you.' he called up with a grin. 'You look a picture.'

'I suppose you better come up,' she said with a resigned sigh.

She disappeared from the window. Hermes heard her clumped down the stairs, throw several bolts on the heavy oak door and fling it open. Aphrodite, Goddes of Love, stood in her dressing gown and slippers in the dingy hall way. She led him up several flights of narrow stairs to her apartment at the top of the building. The place had obviously been the site of much revelry the night before and was a mess.

'Very nice,' said Hermes, a touch of irony in his voice, 'What are the neighbours like ?'

'It suits me fine for my purposes,' said Aphrodite, lighting the kettle and searching around trying to find the coffee.

'And just precisely what is that purpose ?,' asked Hermes.

'Hmm,' snapped Aphrodite, 'What gives you the right to question me ?'

'Come off it cousin, ' said Hermes, 'You know full well I'm carrying out Zeus' instructions, which is what you're supposed to be doing as well. He told you to do everything you could to stop the French President committing his country to war. Instead you've pushed him into invading England, which he had no intention of doing, just so you can continue your feud with Hera.'

Aphrodite knew she dare not risk incurring Zeus' fury by an outright show of defiance and that Hermes was only the messenger boy. 'Well I've only been having a little fun with this Frenchman. I've got them all building this huge tunnel under the sea. And Eros has enjoyed playing here, loosing off arrows all over the city. But I suppose if Zeus really does want me to stop him launching his invasion of England I can do it. I can wind him around my little finger and make him do anything I want.'

'Well you better move fast as well,' said Hermes. 'What is the score, the invasion must be imminent ?'

'President Loubet is coming here tonight for our final rendezvous before he leaves for Calais to supervise the launch of his invasion of England.' replied Aphrodite. 'In fact, he doesn't realise that it was due anyway to be our final meeting, full stop.'

'The poor dear man,' she said, as if she genuinely felt sorry for him. 'For months I've been gradually coaxing him in the secrets of the male erection. Bit by bit, through a mixture of potions and the rigorous course of exercises I've proscribed for him, he's finally reaching the stage where he can achieve a big one and sustain it long enough to be able to do something useful with it. Finally, this is to be the night he's been waiting for all those months, when he actually gets to try it out properly, ahead of his going off to order the greatest French military triumph since the days of Napoleon.'

'I thought I at least owed him that.' said Aphrodite, a little coyly. 'After all that work.'

'All the same to me,' said Hermes. 'But if I was you I wouldn't mention it to Apollo.'

'Hmmm, him,' she scoffed. 'Thinks he owns me.'

'Anyway, much as I'd like to hang around and chat I'm afraid I've got quite a lot on at the moment,' said Hermes. 'Can I tell Zeus that you're confident you can stop your Frenchman ordering his invasion of England and will take responsibility for that.'

'You tell the boss man not to worry,' she said with a smile. 'It will soon be in my capable hands.'

* * *

President Emile Loubet thought he would burst with excitement all day. How could one mortal man be expected to contain the thrill of such splendours. Tonight he was finally due to take his beautiful goddess into his arms and know that ecstasy he had only been able to dream about all his life. Then to top it all he would ride away into the dawn to lead the French nation in its most glorious ever victory against France's most ancient and persistent enemy, England.

'Charlemagne, Napoleon, ...and LOUBET,' thought Loubet. 'The three greatest Frenchmen that ever lived. Ha Ha Ha ! I feel like a god.'

During the special rigorous exercises he'd been forced to conduct to strengthen his erection, on the hour, without fail, every sixty minutes for the past six months he'd often felt a little less than godly. He'd had many embarrassing moments when he'd been caught exercising it after having to make some limp excuse to pop out from some cabinet meeting, or military planning session, or suchlike. He had hoped people hadn't guessed what it was he was doing when he might have been seen by some secretary or official but it had reached his ears that this apparently strange behaviour of his had resulted in him being given some new nickname, but he didn't know what that was.

'Anyway, why should I care,' thought Loubet. 'Those fools that seem to uncontrollably giggle every time they see me will be singing a different song after tomorrow. The exercises and the potions have worked. I know it works. And tonight will be like no other.'

* * *

Loubet left his guards posted in the hall outside the flat and went in. He could hear the object of his desires preparing dinner in the kitchen and the smell of fresh oysters caught his nostrils. He put the champagne he had bought into the waiting ice bucket and went into the bathroom to shower and change into his bathrobe.

'Well cheri,' he declared, emerging from the bathroom. 'Tonight is the greatest of all nights. Let us drink to our love, a love that for future generations will eclipse that of even Antony and Cleopatra.' He popped the cork suggestively out of the champagne bottle with a sly wink and poured two glasses.

'I remember her,' thought Aphrodite. 'She had talent for a mortal.'

'Emile, my hero,' she said, lifting her glass to his toast. 'So how is it my dear. Have you been keeping up your exercises. Does it work.'

'Mon cheri,' he cried triumphantly, 'it works. It works. See...'

And he jumped up and parted his bathrobe to reveal his gloriously erect member throbbing like a beacon. His white beard parted by a smile from ear to ear.

'Well hush my mouth,' said the girl in appreciation. 'Emile, you have worked hard. That's a whopper.'

'Yes, and so firm,' he squealed in delight. 'Come to me my darling,' he said and stretched out his arms.

'Oh well,' thought Aphrodite and she started to rise.

Just then the door of the flat burst inwards off its hinges with a mighty crash and there in the empty doorway stood a tall figure dressed in the garb of a market porter, his striped shirt stretched over a muscular chest and shoulders, long blond hair radiating out beneath his beret, and his eyes glowering with fury at the President, his erect penis and the girl.

'What are you doing with my wife ?,' screamed the intruder.

'I'm not his wife,' protested the girl. 'Pol go away, you'll ruin everything.'

'Guards, guards…!,' screamed the President.

Loubet looked beyond the figure to the hallway. His guards were nowhere to be seen and the hall was unaccountably empty but for a number of frogs hopping around.

'I told you what I'd do to this fool if I caught you messing around with him,' spat the furious Apollo.

'My good man, I assure you…..,' started Loubet, but Apollo grasped the collars of his bathrobe in one hand, lifted him into the air as if he were no more than a rag doll, and hurled him unceremoniously across the room, fortunately for the President to land on the sofa some fifteen feet away.

Aphrodite rushed between them and put her hands on Apollo's shoulders to calm him down. 'Please Pol, you musn't hurt him. I'm only carrying out Zeus' orders. I swear nothing happened between us yet' she pleaded.

'Sod Zeus and his orders,' bellowed Apollo. 'I want you. I want you now. And I'm going to turn that little French turd into a frog.'

Loubet, his head still spinning, could make little sense of what was going on around him. He looked into the eyes of the terrifying figure standing glowering above him and a fear like nothing he had never known before pierced the very core of his soul. As he stared transfixed by those fiery eyes he felt himself and his surroundings slipping away. He was descending into some cold, dark, watery world where sinister eyes and teeth lurked behind every shadow.

'No Apollo stop,' Aphrodite begged, 'I'll come with you. We'll leave here. Just let him go.'

Loubet felt himself being dragged back from some unspeakable depths. He was on the sofa again, looking up at his assailant, who was now cuddling the girl. Strangely he felt no jealousy nor the slightest tinge of affection anymore for this girl who had so obsessed his every waking moment for more than six months. Only an abject terror at whatever it was he had just experienced.

Apollo looked up from his embrace. 'Get out of here,' he snapped.

The President didn't need telling twice. Barefoot, his bathrobe flapping around his naked backside, he was out of the room, down the stairs, into the street and, with his confused guardsman following on behind, he didn't stop running until he reached the Elysee Palace.

'Oh Apollo,' said Aphrodite, 'you're a sentimental old fool.'

'Listen baby,' said Apollo, 'I've had enough of all this business with Zeus, Poseidon and Ares. From what I can see its a pity the old man ever had to wake up. This city might be nice now but I reckon things are pretty soon going to start hotting up around here and I for one would rather be out of the way when it does. So how's about you'n me just taking off to this beautiful unspoilt tropical island I've discovered in the Indian Ocean, far away from all this so-called civilisation where we can leave them all to get on with their war in peace.'

'Apollo that sounds just heavenly,' she cooed and she fell into his embrace.

* * *

Back at the Elysee Palace a bath and a little lie down had helped President Loubet start to recover slightly from his harrowing experience earlier that evening. But there was no time to lose. His thoughts were no longer on the girl. Instead they were now focused firmly on the task ahead. He changed into his best dress uniform and proudly descended into the courtyard where a fine white stallion and a guard of honour were waiting to escort him to Calais where at dawn he would order the invasion of Britain.

Chapter Ten

Captain Hans Job of the Imperial Guard had become the toast of Berlin society and Heracles had been enjoying himself no end since he had accepted the Kaiser's commission six months earlier. His official duties were light, largely just to follow Wilhelm around and look smart when he attended official ceremonies, but his private role as the Kaiser's favourite and confidant had ensured him virtually unlimited grace and favour everywhere he went. Best of all he had been delighted to discover that his very own creation, the Olympic Games, had been recently revived and the hopes of the German fatherland to outshine every other nation at the next Olympiad due to take place in 1904 in the strange new land of America were now confidently riding on their new athletic super hero.

Heracles never rose before 7 am when his breakfast would be served by whichever buxom fraulien or frau from the small army of such ladies who idolised and doted on him had been lucky enough to be selected for his favour the previous night. After a couple of hours workout in the military gymnasium he would then attend on the Kaiser, who was increasingly pre-occupied with his General Staff on their plans to invade France. Most afternoons would be spent fussing around Wilhelm, listening to his little worries and misgivings about the coming war and making sure that his resolve stayed solid. The evenings were largely his own and Hans Job exploited his almost divine celebrity status with corresponding energy and enthusiasm in the most fashionable salons of Berlin.

But finally, after all those months of preparation the great day was at hand. Tomorrow morning a special elite division of the German army that had been secretly assembled west of Bonn would, on the Kaiser's signal, cross the Belgium border at Liege, sweeping aside any scant Belgium resistance, and then race the 175 miles to Paris along the north banks of the Meuse and Oise rivers, hopefully securing the French capital by the end of the second day and before the unsuspecting French armies, all largely deployed to the east and south along their border with Germany, would have time to react.

At the same time, and vital to the plan, special coded instructions would be issued that would mobilise for sudden war the entire German army of over half a million men, plucking brigades and garrisons from all over Germany and channelling them via a complex series of railway schedules through the breech made in the French northern front and to resist a French counterattack into Alsace and Lorraine.

Heracles had been quite fascinated at how detailed and complicated the business of warfare had become in the few decades since Poseidon and Ares had started to stir things up. Thirty years earlier, when Germany had last invaded France via largely the same route, relatively small opposing armies relying almost exclusively on horse and man power alone had clashed at the battle of Sedan, the German army won the day, and that was largely the end of the war but for a messy drawn out siege of Paris. Now things were quite a bit different. Germany and France shared about equally well over one million men in their regular armies now equipped with huge steel armaments and high explosives.

With the logistical considerations involved in operating and fighting with such large forces military planners everywhere, and especially in Germany, had become increasingly pre-occupied with the question of mobilisation. Basically, with the resources that had been available during the Franco-Prussian War it would maybe take months to pull together and effectively launch an entire such army, by which time your adversary would be tipped off and have plenty of time to deploy his forces and benefit from the increasing advantage the massive fire power of the new weapons would bestow to a prepared defender. The big difference now though was the extensive development of the railway system, still only in its infancy in 1870.

The railway system made it feasible to mobilise and launch mass armies within perhaps a few days instead of weeks and increasingly the speed with which they could mobilise their army came to obsess the German High Command. The key to success lay in the efficiency of their railway timetable scheduling which was elevated to an art and a science, almost a religion, by the German planners.

At all cost the Germans wanted to avoid their entire army getting bogged down in a bloody stand-off with the French without achieving their objective of capturing Paris. Surprise and speed was of the essence, which was why the assault would be opened by a smaller force of some 50,000 men which had been deployed secretly across Germany's border with Belgium whilst the rest of the army remained in their peace time positions across Germany so as not to alert the French. Once the opening attack and drive on Paris had begun the Kaiser would then issue by telegraph a series of coded messages to military units throughout the German Empire that would swing into action the detailed logistical plans which, after all their work and effort on the timetables, they were confident would beat France to the draw in the great game of mobilisation.

It was Captain Hans Job's special honour and privilege to guard the attaché case, containing these coded instructions that would launch half a million men into war, when he escorted the Kaiser to the battle front that evening. After lunch he and the Kaiser, together with the military top brass, were due to inspect a special new German secret weapon which was to be used in the war against France for the first time ever. Hans was due to receive the case of instructions, codenamed the Railway Timetables, after this meeting when he would then travel by train with Wilhelm to Bonn ready for him to launch the assault force and mobilise the German army the following morning.

Heracles lay back in the sumptuous silks sheets, plucked a grape from his breakfast tray and playfully slapped the blonde pigtailed wench that was laying beside him on her fleshy rump. He wondered what this secret weapon might be. Normally Wilhelm blurted everything out to him but the Kaiser, clearly infatuated himself with this new tool of war, had insisted on making a big secret about it, promising Hans he was in for a special treat when he saw it that afternoon. The little ornate gold carriage clock on the marble mantle piece chimed seven o'clock. Time to rise.

* * *

Heracles joined the Kaiser in his coach on the journey to the top secret military base 20 miles outside Berlin while the rest of the escort rode behind. Wilhelm babbled incessantly the whole way; about the glory the war would bring him, his glorious new secret weapon, the glory Hans would win for Germany at the Olympic Games, and how Germany under his leadership was set to become the world's leading nation in this new century. Heracles thought he would scream at one stage, but curbed his impulse to grab the Kaiser and physically hurl him from the coach.

None to soon for Heracles they eventually reached the base. While the remainder of the guards waited at the main barracks Heracles joined the Kaiser on horseback to ride to an obscure group of buildings at one corner of the base dominated by a huge corrugated metal construction resembling a giant barn. A pair of doors spanned one side of the barn and in front of these waited the three most powerful men in Germany after the Kaiser himself; Prince von Bulow, the German Chancellor; Admiral von Tirpitz, the architect of Germany's naval build-up; and Count von Schlieffen, Chief of the General Staff, whose cherished master plan for the swift defeat of France was finally to become a reality in the morning.

'Greetings, your Majesty,' called up von Bulow.

Wilhelm gave the group a cursory wave, dismounted and enthusiastically approached a smaller, moustachioed man in civilian dress standing with them who Heracles didn't recognise.

'My dear Ferdinand,' beamed the Kaiser, 'Always a pleasure to see you. How's our little baby coming along.'

'Thank you your Majesty,' replied Ferdinand, 'She's performing beautifully sir, as I hope to shortly demonstrate.'

'Excellent, excellent,' said the Kaiser, rubbing his hands. 'Hans, allow me to introduce Count Ferdinand von Zeppelin, the genius behind our new master weapon.'

Von Zeppelin clicked his heels together and nodded his head a little towards Heracles. 'An honour to meet the great athlete and darling of the German people,' he said, a touch sarcastically Heracles felt and he thought he saw a thin little smile pass across von Schlieffen's lips.

'Watch it, buddy,' Heracles thought to himself, but smiled sweetly back at the Count.

'Hans, prepare yourself for a most wondrous sight,' said the Kaiser, who nodded to von Zeppelin, who waved to a group of overalled men who began to pull open the huge metal doors.

Heracles was indeed full of wonder at what he saw. In fact, he wondered whether or not Kaiser and the entire German Staff had gone stark raving mad. There before him, filling the empty building was a colossal grey penis. A huge cloth covered structure shaped like a fat cigar, some 500 feet long and 40 feet wide stood erect above him. Below this hung two huge metal testicles, with one painfully twisted forward of the other. Through windows in the testicles Heracles could see men moving about in white overalls and he wondered whether they were suppose to represent sperms.

The group looked on at Heracles expectantly, waiting for his reaction. He really couldn't quite think what to say. Eventually he stumbled out, 'Well that should certainly frighten the French President.'

'Indeed, indeed.' quipped the Kaiser.

Then the penny dropped. 'Of course,' said Heracles, 'I get it. Brilliant. You leave the giant penis outside the gates of Paris and go away. The French, thinking its some kind of god or fertility symbol, drag it into the city, then, later that night, out of the testicles come the concealed German soldiers, throw open the gates and....'

'Hans, what on earth are you babbling about penises and testicles for, don't you realise what this is ?,' asked the Kaiser. The vons all turned their heads to conceal their sneers and Heracles felt himself blushing a little.

'Er, ...no.' he confessed.

'Ho ho ho, I love your peasant simplicity, Hans,' laughed the Kaiser, throwing his head back and making his eagle wobble precariously atop his helmet, 'Its an airship, a flying machine.'

'You mean mortals, er, I mean men, can now fly ?' asked Heracles who hadn't been aware of this new and most incredible wonder.

'That's right,' interrupted von Zeppelin. 'In fact, balloons full of gas or hot air have been used to haul people aloft for some time but only recently have proper airships that can steer and propel themselves been developed. The French think that they are the leaders in this field and have been trying to build an airship of their own under the direction of a Brazilian named Alberto Santos-Dumont. This year one of his airships circled the Eiffel Tower, but unbeknownst to them, the French effort is far behind that of the fatherland's.'

'The French airships can barely steer themselves or perform in even light winds. My airships incorporate the latest technology and can fly higher, faster and longer, and carry a far greater payload, than anything the French or anybody else is even dreaming of developing,' continued von Zeppelin, evidently having got onto his favourite subject. 'The airship carries two of the new petroleum driven Daimler internal combustion engines which can deliver the power of thirty horses to the twin propellers to push the craft forward at speeds of up to 20 miles an hour. The giant bag contains within its rigid frame seventeen individual cells of special rubberised cloth carrying well over a million litres of hydrogen gas which can lift the ship and its payload some two thousand feet into the air...'

'This weapon will make Germany the master of all Europe,' von Tirpitz cut in. 'In this airship we can fly like gods high above enemy armies, battleships or cities, out of effective range from any rifle fire from the ground, and drop bombs on them at will. The only thing that could possibly ever challenge it would be another airship and, as the Count has explained, our qualitative lead in airship design is such that we could blast any type of craft any enemy could conceivably put up against us out of the sky long before it could get close enough to threaten us.'

'Truly in this new century the nature of warfare will be like never before,' said von Schlieffen. 'For thousands of years man has fought by land and sea. From now on though a new dimension will be opened up. Control of the sky itself will be the decisive factor in future wars. The airship is set to be the supreme, invincible weapon of war and in the twentieth century Germany will rule the skies as Britain has ruled the waves in the last century.'

Heracles could see that the German top brass were all pretty fired up about this new weapon and, he had to admit, if what they were saying was true; that it could cross borders and seas at will, high above and invulnerable to the enemy forces who would be like helpless ants far below waiting for a giant foot to fall; then this might indeed make the German Empire master of the whole continent.

Whilst the Kaiser and Heracles stayed with von Zeppelin to watch the airship being marshalled out of the hanger ready to begin its trials the other three vons returned to the main barracks to prepare the case containing the coded mobilisation instructions, which the Kaiser's personal bodyguard was due to escort with him to the battlefront.

As they entered an office von Schlieffen noticed a young lieutenant of the Imperial Guard in the corridor. 'You, come here,' he barked at him.

He was a strong, handsome young man von Schlieffen noted although strangely a little short for an Imperial Guardsman. 'Obviously someone's favourite,' he thought, also now noticing the poor fit of his uniform which looked too large for him. Still, he didn't have time to worry about that sort of thing now.'

'Stand guard by this door,' he ordered. 'Don't let anybody enter.'

'Jawohl !,' the lieutenant snapped back and jumped to attention outside the door as von Schlieffen joined the other two inside.

Hermes was glad that they hadn't entered the next office, where they would have found a naked, sleeping guardsman whose uniform he had just borrowed.

Although Hermes could still strip off, don his winged boots and helmet and take to the sky when the need arose, these days he preferred conventional garb and means of transport when he went amongst mortals. He also found flying under his own power a lot of effort and the trip from to Berlin from Paris where he had left Aphrodite earlier that day had near worn him out but had been vital if he was to succeed in his mission to stop the war. He moved his ear closer to the door so that he could hear what they were saying.

'That oaf actually thought that the airship was a giant penis. Its deplorable that the Kaiser himself, the helmsman of the German nation, should be so enthralled by this licentious peasant soldier,' declared von Bulow.

'Even my pretty little Gretchen has been sucked into his web debauchery,' protested von Schlieffen, 'Like all of the women and most of the men of Germany he's bewitched everybody with this athletic hero nonsense.'

'If only Bismarck was still with us,' bemoaned von Tirpitz, 'He'd know what to do about it.'

'Well we know what to do about it. I trust that we are all still agreed, gentlemen ?,' said von Bulow solemnly.

'Agreed,' said von Schlieffen.

'For the Fatherland,' declared von Tirpitz.

'Is that it ?,' asked von Bulow.

'Yes,' replied von Schlieffen.

'And the other one ?'

'I'll take care of that.'

Hermes wasn't quite sure who or what was being referred to here.

'Gentlemen,' announced von Bulow proudly, 'Tomorrow morning at dawn two glorious blows will be struck for the future of German Empire. Our armies will sweep away the French enemy beyond our borders and at the same time this degenerate cancer threatening the heart of our nation at home will be removed.'

'Is everything set ?,' asked von Tirpitz.

'Yes,' said von Schlieffen. 'Tomorrow morning Captain Hans Job is in for a little surprise when he gets his breakfast.'

Just then there was a little commotion in the hallway as the Kaiser, followed by Heracles, entered the building booming, 'Where are they then ? They're ready to start the trials soon.'

Von Bulow appeared at the door. 'Here Your Majesty,' he called. 'May the General, the Admiral and I just have a moment of your time to discuss final procedures for transmitting the mobilisation orders tomorrow morning. As you are aware this is absolutely vital to our battle plan.'

'Oh all right, quickly then,' he huffed, entering the room. 'Wait here Hans.'

'Hi there Hek,' Hermes called cheerfully to his Captain after they had closed the door.

'What in Hades are you doing here ?,' roared Heracles, trying to keep his voice down and resisting them temptation to grab Hermes and carry out his threat to pull his head off.

'What do you think. Boss man's orders,' replied Hermes, standing his ground.

'What orders,' snapped Heracles.

'Look pal,' said Hermes, squaring up to the giant, 'You know as well as I do that Zeus sent you to Germany with the aim of stopping the Kaiser going to war. Instead you've actually provoked him into ordering a war and then for the last six months you've just been sitting back enjoying being worshipped as an athletic hero.'

'Its been just liked old times,' beamed Heracles. 'I'm even going to compete in the Olympic Games again, can you believe it.'

'Well the choice is yours buddy,' said Hermes. 'I've got a great deal to do yet if I'm going to carry out Zeus's orders to stop all the great powers of Europe from rushing into war with each other in the morning and I'm already well behind schedule. You can either help me, in which case you're in the clear, or I can let Zeus know that you've decided to disobey him and throw your lot in with Poseidon and Ares.'

'Now hang on a minute, ' protested Heracles who, whatever else he might have been planning he wasn't planning to take on the king of the gods, 'I've just been amusing myself. I've got nothing to do with those two.'

'Oh, and I wouldn't be too sure about competing in the Olympic Games if I was you,' added Hermes. 'Your new found friends are planning to assassinate you in the morning.'

'Whhatt..?,' asked Heracles.

'Its right,' said Hermes. 'I just overheard them. I think they're planning to poison your breakfast.'

'The Bastards,' spat Heracles.

'So what's it going to be big fella ?,' asked Hermes.

'O.k. Partners,' said Heracles, clutching Hermes hand in his great paw. 'I was getting bored with all this anyway. So what's the plan ?'

'I'm not sure yet,' confided Hermes. 'All we can do is hang around and try to find some way of putting a spanner into their war plans. Trouble is I've done nothing yet to stop the war from starting in the east. I've got a plan that might work there, but it involves getting to Bulgaria, which is nearly a thousand miles from here, by the morning. I don't think I could even manage it myself so soon after flying here from Paris, but it would be pretty vital, for reasons I'll explain later, that both of us went there.'

'Hmmm..., said Heracles, trying to think of a plan; and failing.

'What are they supposed to be doing now,' asked Hermes.

'Well, in a minute I've got to take charge of the coded instructions to order the German armies' mobilisation from von Schlieffen, we go and see the airship take off, and then the Kaiser and I leave by train for the front where he's due to launch the invasion in the morning,' said Heracles.

'That's it,' declared Hermes, suddenly jumping up, 'I knew Moros himself, the supreme power to whom even Zeus is subject, was with us.'

Just then the office door opened and the Kaiser called for Hans.

'Just do as I say,' Hermes whispered to Heracles.

'Captain, it is your honour and privilege to guard these documents, which with the Kaiser's authority are to be presented to the communications officer at battlefield headquarters in the morning once the opening attack has begun. The contents of this case are crucial to the German invasion plans. You must guard them with your life and never let them leave your side,' von Schlieffen announced as he handed Heracles the sacred attaché case.

'Right, can we go and see the airship take off now,' insisted the Kaiser.

Hermes followed the party back to the Zeppelin shed unseen. They stopped in front of the giant craft, now out in the open. The behemoth stood tethered to the ground by a large rope with its propellers gently turning, keeping its two aluminium pods hovering just above the ground. Besides each pod stood two overalled technicians, waiting for the order to enter the craft and begin trials.

Hermes crept in behind Heracles, concealed by his great bulk and whispered in his ear.

'Now,' he shouted, and he rushed forward scattering the crew like ninepins and leapt into the doorway of the control cabin. At the same instant Heracles, still clutching the attaché case, rushed to the front of the craft, grabbed with one hand the huge metal ring to which the airship's rope was tethered and, to the amazement of those who watched, ripped the ring from the ground.

Heracles rushed back underneath the gasbag as it slowly started to lift above him, bound twenty feet into the air to grab Hermes's hand as he hung out of the cabin doorway. Before the stunned audience could gather their wits and comprehend what had happened the two were aboard the airship as it lifted into the sky above them, its dazed crew sprawling on the ground in its diminishing shadow.

As the terrible realisation started to dawn Wilhelm almost collapsed in a heap. He started to sob , 'Oh My God, Oh My God....,' over and over again. Count von Zeppelin stood frozen in disbelief. The three vons huddled together and began urgently conferring.

Finally von Bulow approached the trembling Kaiser. 'Your Majesty, all is not lost,' he said firmly.

'What do you mean,' bawled the Kaiser, 'Hans was a traitor, obviously working for the French and after our new wonder weapon all along. Now he's not only got that but he's got the vital instructions we need to mobilise the army and he'll be able to spill our invasion plans to the French.'

'Your Majesty, it may look bad, but its not all as it may seem,' took up von Schlieffen. 'Please permit me to explain. German Military Intelligence has suspected this Hans Job of being an enemy agent all along. All his communications have been monitored from the day he joined your Imperial Guard, of which there have been surprisingly few other than requisitions for food, wine and ale. We are confident that none of our war plans have been conveyed to the French.'

'But he'll fly there now, in the airship, and tell them,' persisted the Kaiser.

'Majesty,' said von Tirpitz. 'The train that will shortly convey you to the border with Belgium will be travelling at up to three times the speed that even our airships are yet capable of. Even assuming these fools know how to fly the thing properly it would take them at best 20 hours to reach the French border from here. Long before then our invasion will be under way.

In any case there's not nearly enough fuel on board for them to travel that far or even leave Germany. We simply need to track the craft and when they are forced to come down we will have both them and the airship. Isn't that right, Count ?'

'Er, yes, I suppose so,' replied von Zeppelin.

'But the mobilisation codes ?,' asked the Kaiser, turning to von Schlieffen.

'Majesty,' he replied, 'Because of our fears that this Hans Job was an enemy agent the General Staff decided that it would be unwise to entrust into his keeping something so important as the Railway Timetables. Everything has gone according to plan. We had expected all along to flush him out by giving him bogus plans; admittedly we weren't expecting him to steal an airship, but as von Tirpitz has explained, we should recover that well inside German territory. I myself have the genuine set of coded instructions, Majesty, and will personally escort you to the front with them.'

'So the invasion can still go ahead ?,' asked Wilhelm, starting to brighten up a little.

'Yes Majesty, most definitely,' stated von Bulow.

'And Hans ?,' he asked, almost a tremor of sorrow shaking his voice as he said the name.

'I swear on my oath as a German officer that he and his accomplice will be dead by the morning,' said von Schlieffen grimly.

* * *

Chapter Eleven

On the 31st March 1901 sunlight broke from the Hampshire Downs to the east, chasing away the last night-time shadows across the flat expanse of Salisbury Plain and illuminated the scene below for a giant golden eagle as he passed across the dawn sky. From far beneath him his keen ears started to pick up the discordant notes of hundreds of bugles from the many army encampments, all carefully concealed from any nearby roads and prying eyes and visible only to the birds. As he passed overhead the eagle observed countless soldiers rousing from their huts and begin to shape themselves into little uniform squares and columns. All were fully laden in battle dress and the many horse drawn wagons starting to load supplies from nearby storehouses confirmed that this was an army on the move.

Wheeling high above the cathedral spires of the ancient city of Salisbury the eagle turned his gaze to the south and discerned the little black outlines of countless cranes framing the port of Southampton and the Solent waterway leading down to the coast. As his course swept him along this channel he spied hundreds of wooden barges moored along both banks, all apparently being readied for some imminent mass boarding. Further along the coast to his left he could see the naval dockyards crammed with numerous battleships of every shape and size.

Across a narrow and crowded stretch of water, still shrouded in a morning mist, lay the diamond-shaped island that was his destination.

* * *

After her little trick with the British Prime Minister the previous summer Hera had found it convenient to use her powers to secure for herself the position of personal private secretarial assistant to the ageing Queen Victoria. In addition to enjoying the trappings of royalty the Queen of the Gods had also found it a particularly good vantage point from which to keep her eye on everything whilst still staying out of the way. Not only did her position allow her to keep tags on the movements of the Prince and Princess of Wales; useful if she had ever needed to impersonate the Princess again; but best of all the British government sent boxes full of stuff to the Queen every day, wherever she was, detailing every little decision and plan they made. Since the old Queen, already in her nineties, senile and slowly deteriorating, had little use for the boxes Hera couldn't quite understand why they bothered, but it allowed her to make sure that there was going to be no backsliding on their plans to invade France.

In fact, this had been a little disrupted a couple of months earlier when the long reign of Queen Victoria finally expired. The old Queen had died at Osborne House on the Isle of Wight late in January. Hera had been in attendance at the time and had managed to stay on to look after the building pending a decision by the new royal family over its future. Although she no longer received the government despatches this was no serious problem. By then she was confident that the British government were firmly committed to the war aims she had given them and, especially with the old woman now out of the way, this seemed like an excellent spot from which to view her armada set sail on its mission to teach Aphrodite a lesson she wouldn't easily forget.

She was quite unaware that holed up in a dark, dank cave not fifteen miles away to the south sat the brooding figure of Poseidon, who had quite separately also selected this island as an ideal vantage point to view the coming carnage. Unlike the refined meal of toast, scones and Scottish marmalade from ornate silver servers and fine tea drunk from the finest porcelain on which the Queen of the Gods breakfasted that morning the god of the sea contented himself on his favourite meal of raw fish.

Hera's breakfast was interrupted by a thunderous knocking on the main door in the hall below and the sound of her butler arguing with someone. 'Who in Hades can that be ?,' she cursed to herself. Shortly the aged butler gingerly entered her breakfast room.

'Milady,' he said nervously. 'There's a person at the door, he looks like an old fisherman, who insists on seeing you. I told him that would be quite impossible at this hour of the day and without a formal appointment, but he's very insistent.'

'What ?,' spat Hera. 'How dare he ? How dare you ? I don't care who he is. Call the constable and get him locked up, whoever he is. Such impudence. I told you I didn't want to be disturbed by anyone for the next twenty-four hours.'

'Yes, Milady. Very good, Milady,' stammered the butler. 'But, but...'

'But what ? Spit it out, you fool,' demanded the furious deity.

'He says he's your husband, Milady,' spluttered the cowering butler.

Hera suddenly froze as if hit by a lightning bolt and then started coughing as she choked on the morsel of toast she had been eating.

'Show him into the study,' she wheezed. 'Tell him I'll be right down.'

* * *

'Darling,' Hera intoned, as she grandly entered the room, 'how wonderful of you to come and visit me. Though its been so quiet and peaceful around here that I was thinking of returning to Olympus soon.'

Zeus stood with his back to her, arms folded behind him, staring through the window at a small yacht moored outside. His straggly hair and beard beneath a battered old skipper's cap and great bulk neatly fitting in to the image of an old sea dog that he had adopted.

'Quiet and peaceful, eh ?,' he finally said. 'That's not the impression I got on my way here this morning. It looks to me like they're all getting ready to go off to war somewhere. Know anything about that by any chance ?'

'I can't think what they might be doing,' said Hera, starting to get a little nervous. 'I must admit though, I've been a little out of touch recently since the old Queen died. Perhaps they are getting up to something but I assure you I know nothing about it.'

'I see,' said Zeus. 'So you know nothing about the Princess of Wales threatening to divorce her husband, the new king, unless the British government agreed to go to war with France ?'

'Oh that,' said Hera, waving a hand in the air and attempting to laugh it off. 'That was just a little joke I played on them last year. The English always play jokes with each other for 1st April. I never thought they'd actually go through with it.'

Zeus stood silently, his back still to her, staring out to sea.

'Oh, my dear...,' she said. 'No. Don't tell me they're actually going to do it. Oh, how could they be so foolish. Oh Darling, how can you forgive me ?'

Zeus had been running through some ideas for a particularly appropriate punishment for his wife's latest act of disobedience. Once in the past he'd bound her in unbreakable golden chains and suspended her from the sky with heavy anvils tied to her feet but in this new age he felt he was going to have to come up with something a little more imaginative. Still, for the moment he felt he better try to keep her on board. He still had Poseidon to deal with and he and Hera had come pretty close once before to overpowering him with the help of Apollo and Athene, for which failed attempt they'd all been roundly punished.

'Well you'd better get them to call it all off,' he said finally, 'and depending on how well you manage that I'll decide whether or not I can forgive you.'

Hera could feel those ghastly anvils dragging on her feet and her body painfully stretching. 'Darling, of course I'll do anything I can,' she said. 'But I don't really know what I can do now at this stage if, as you say, they're already on the move.'

'Well you can do what you did before. You can impersonate the new Queen only this time get them to call off the attack,' said Zeus. 'And you'd better get on the case pretty damned fast. Their invasion force is set to sail after midnight tonight. You'll need to get to London and persuade the government to call the whole thing off by this afternoon. Its a long way for a peacock'

Hera wasn't sure whether or not Zeus had bought her story, that she hadn't seriously wanted these fools to invade France, but she felt she'd better go along with his instructions now.

'I'll do it, my darling,' she said. 'You can rely on me. I'll put to rights any problem that, in my silly innocence, I might have unwittingly caused and then you'll forgive me.'

'See that you do,' said Zeus solemnly. 'And now, I'd like to borrow that yacht you have moored out there.'

* * *

Big Ben was striking four o'clock by the time Hera, once again having assumed the appearance of the, now Queen, Alexandra swept into Downing Street demanding to see the Prime Minister urgently. To her annoyance she had been asked to wait like some commoner in an anteroom a full thirty minutes and she was starting to get a little nervous that somebody might tumble the parallel existence of the real Queen, who she hoped would be safely tucked away in Windsor Castle.

Finally she was led into the cabinet room where she found Lord Salisbury seated with the Cabinet Secretary and four others. On his right hand sat Salisbury's nephew and political heir apparent Arthur Balfour, government leader in the House of Commons, and to his right Joseph Chamberlain, the Colonial Secretary. These three were the most senior and powerful members of the government but Hera failed to recognise the pokey-looking pair seated away to the left of the table.

'Your Royal Highness,' said Salisbury, rising and bowing as the title demanded, 'I regret that this really is a most busy time for His Majesty's Government. I must ask you to be brief and, if necessary, we can arrange a more formal audience when we have a little more time available.'

'Prime Minister,' snorted the Queen, looking around her and down her nose at the assembled group, 'what I have to say to you is of a most confidential nature. I would appreciate speaking to you in private.'

The old man stood his ground. 'I regret, Your Highness, that would be most improper,' he replied. 'You know young Arthur and Mr Chamberlain, of course, and the Cabinet Secretary. These two gentlemen, Doctor Barnet and Doctor Plate, are government employees bound to official secrecy. Anything you may have to say to me in my capacity as Prime Minister you may freely discuss here.'

'Very well,' she snapped back. 'What's happening over your plans to invade France ?'

The politicians shot nervous glances between themselves. 'Your

Highness,' replied Salisbury, 'You'll appreciate that this is a most sensitive issue. But everything is going ahead as planned. At midnight our troops will start embarking onto a fleet of specially constructed barges that, even as we speak, are being readied in the Solent. The Royal Navy will escort the invasion force across the Channel for dawn landings on the French coast. By midnight tomorrow we expect to have captured Paris. Mr Chamberlain, Arthur and I are shortly due to travel to Portsmouth by train to supervise the launch of the fleet so, as you may imagine, we really are rather pressed at the moment.'

'Then there's still time,' said Hera, more to herself.

'Still time,' repeated Salisbury. 'Time for what.'

'I want you to call it off,' she said firmly. 'Call off the invasion.'

'What ?,' thundered Chamberlain, visibly starting to shake with rage. Balfour looked at his uncle nervously.

'Your Highness,' said Salisbury calmly, 'that really is ridiculous. You simply can't order the government around in this manner. After nine months of planning we have 100,000 men ready to march. We can't possibly call it off.'

'You'd better call it off if you know what's good for you,' insisted Hera, starting to get very angry. 'Becoming King hasn't made a scrap of difference to Bertie's philandering. Its made the bugger worse. Well I'm not putting up with it any longer. Either you help me out with the little matter of calling off the invasion of France or that's it, I sue him for divorce. And you know what that will mean for your precious British Empire.'

'I'm sorry you said that, Your Highness,' replied the sombre Prime Minister. 'I regret that fortunes of the Empire cannot be held hostage to the whims of an, obviously deranged, jealous old woman.'

'What...?,' gasped the Queen in astonishment at such insolence. 'How dare you.'

'Your Highness,' continued Salisbury, 'Doctors Barnet and Plate are fully qualified to immediately certify you as insane and in need of urgent treatment. If you persist with these outrageous threats then we will have no choice but to place you in immediate protective custody and transfer you to a secure government run institution where your treatment can begin. Stop this nonsense now and we needn't go ahead. But I warn you, you will be watched constantly by the secret service and any future deviation of this nature will be swiftly dealt with.'

Hera stood frozen considering the implications of what she had just heard and curbing her immediate impulse to lash out and turn them all into a herd of swine. That would create too big a sensation which Zeus certainly wouldn't like. But clearly the game was up. She couldn't go ahead without her impersonation soon being exposed and clearly they weren't quite as stupid, or were at least prepared to be more ruthless in the protection of their monarchical institutions, than she had imagined.

'Damn them,' she cursed to herself. 'Let them have their damn war then. The fools have no idea what it is they're getting into. Its not my fault. I tried my best to stop them. Zeus will just have to accept that.'

Feigning genuine remorse she meekly responded, 'Prime Minister, gentlemen, I'm sorry. I really don't know what came over me. Of course I don't want to divorce the King. And I'm quite happy to see you bashing the frogs. I think I'll retire to Windsor now and stop wasting any more of your time when you're obviously so busy.'

'There, there, Your Highness,' said a consolatory and relieved Salisbury. 'I understand that you ladies have, well, your little phases. Nothing to worry about. You return to Windsor and we can put all this behind us. May I arrange an escort ?'

'That's quite all right, thank you, I have my own,' she said and she took her leave.

'Brilliant, uncle,' quipped Balfour after she had left. 'Just as you predicted it worked.'

'I still think we should have had her shot and blamed it on anarchists,' snapped Chamberlain. 'Much safer that way. How d'you know she's not going to just bring all this up again in a month's time ?'

'Well it may have to come to that in the end,' said Salisbury, 'but for the moment we'll have the Queen watched night and day. I don't want her so much as filling her chamber pot without a report about it on my desk the next morning.'

Turning to the Cabinet Secretary he demanded, 'How is it we got no word in advance from our agents at Windsor that she was on her way here. Have them all fired and replace them with professionals. And double their numbers.'

* * *

Chapter Twelve

At first Hermes and Heracles inside the Zeppelin were simply lifted into the air above the military base. As they looked down upon the distraught Kaiser and his entourage, growing ever smaller as the ground beneath them grew ever larger and further away, the light breeze began to push the airship away to the east. Soon they were over a thousand feet above the ground with the seemingly endless, flat North German Plain all around them glimmering in the afternoon sunlight.

Heracles noticed a river winding below them running from the south towards the coastline he could see far to the north. It resembled a thin golden thread or the track of a snail shining in the sunlight as it snaked its way across the plains towards the distant mountains to the south where lay its source.

'That's the River Oder,' Hermes informed him, 'We need to follow that southwards and then aim at the gap between the Alps and the Carpathians. From there it should be pretty easy to pick up the Danube and follow that to our destination in Bulgaria.'

'You still haven't told me why its so important that we go to this place Bulgaria, wherever in Hades that is,' said Heracles.

'I'll tell you in a minute, Hek,' said Hermes. 'First I better find out how we drive this thing.'

Hermes inspected the controls, which to Heracles looked like a confusing mass of pulleys and levers, and he made a brief aerial inspection of the other pod and the airship's exterior. He returned to the control cabin and began manipulating the levers.

'Quite straightforward really,' he said smugly. 'This lever controls the big vertical rudder at the back which tells the ship which direction to go.'

Hermes pulled the lever full over to the left. Heracles heard the creaking of pulleys and a felt a little movement in the airship's frame as the large rudder at the rear of the craft responded. Slowly the nose of the huge craft began to turn southwards and when he was nicely aligned with the river Hermes returned the lever to its starting position to set a course dead ahead.

He then tinkered with some knobs on the engine. 'Might as well put the foot down and see what this baby can do flat out,' he said, and the pitch of their hum rose as the two huge pairs of propellers either side of the ship began to speed up.

'So, that's left, right and forward sorted out,' said Hermes, 'now what about up and down.'

He tinkered around a little more. 'I see,' he said finally. 'These controls allow you to release gas to eventually bring the airship down. And these controls then must...'

Hermes quickly turned all the levers full over. A shudder rumbled across the airframe. Huge sections opened up along its base as a mass of dust and debris billowed out underneath them and Heracles felt himself and the ship suddenly grabbed and flung upwards as if by some invisible hand. He thought the cocky young fool must have blown up the craft.

'...yep, release ballast to give the ship lift,' he continued. 'We might as well have maximum height as well.'

The airship settled down. They were now even higher above the ground and heading south, with Hermes making the odd adjustment on the main rudder to follow the course of the river and frowning over a panel of dials.

'So,' said Heracles finally, 'Why are we; indeed, why am I; going to Bulgaria.'

'Well,' said Hermes, 'Aphrodite has promised to take care of the French President and get him to stop his country's invasion of England. Meanwhile Zeus himself should be visiting England and says he'll look after stopping them from invading the French. So that one's his problem. Now that we've got the German army's mobilisation instructions in that attache case they'll have to postpone their invasion plans. It will take them months to prepare and issue new instructions and they won't risk sending their task force into France if they can't follow that up with a full mobilisation.'

'I don't think I detected the word "Bulgaria" at all then,' said Heracles.

'So that just leaves the Russian, Hapsburg and Ottoman Empires to worry about and all of them are due to stumble into war with each other tomorrow morning in a wild, remote place at the back end of nowhere that goes by the name of Bulgaria,' said Hermes in exasperation.

'Right, and what do we do when we get there then to stop three empires going to war with each other ?,' asked Heracles.

'Well I have a plan,' came the reply.

'Go on then...,' said the giant.

'Bulgaria is the next domino waiting to fall in a process that's been going on for some time in the Balkans as the decadent old Ottoman Empire breaks up in Europe. Its a rugged country peopled by fierce tribesman and the Turkish authorities long ago gave up any hope of successfully collecting any tax revenue from the region. Accordingly, and under pressure from the other powers, they've hitherto given the Bulgarians almost total autonomy to govern themselves, or at least what passes for government, under their own ruler, Prince Ferdinand.'

'However officially Bulgaria, along with Bosnia-Herzegovina which the Austrians are already occupying by treaty, belongs to the Ottoman Empire. Sultan Abdul Hamid, under the influence of Apollo, thinks it is finally time for him to stop the rot at home and abroad with a grand gesture, namely invading the country and re-asserting his authority.'

'Meanwhile though Austrian forces to the west and Russian forces to the east are both poised to send armies into the country and proclaim its independence from Turkey as a fait acompli, both expecting to then incorporate Bulgaria as a satellite state within their own empires.'

'So how are we supposed to stop that from happening then,' asked Heracles, 'If in the morning three separate armies are all due to invade the country from the west, the east and the south.'

'Right, well this is my plan, and why you are vital to it,' said Hermes. 'If we can get to Prince Ferdinand of Bulgaria by the morning and persuade him to take the initiative in proclaiming his own country's independence without any outside help, then this will hopefully forestall the three powers and make them think twice about invading the country.

'But how are we going to persuade the Prince to do that. And anyway, that would only spur the powers on all the more to move in and take over,' said Heracles.

'That's where you come in; and these German officers' uniforms,' replied Hermes. 'Everybody knows who you are, you're the favourite of the Kaiser of Germany. You're also an international star athlete, not to mention a show-off, who's picture has gone all over the world. Ferdinand, who is German born, will certainly know who you are, along with the various Austrian, Russian and Turkish agents at his court. He and everybody else is bound to believe us when we arrive with the message, conveyed by the Kaiser's own right-hand man, that the German Empire will back the total independence of Bulgaria, with force if necessary. That's certain to make them all pull back. Each of the three powers is expecting to pull off a quick coup without facing any serious opposition. None of them are planning to go to war with Germany over Bulgaria.'

'O.k.,' said Heracles. 'So how do we find this Prince Ferdinand.'

'Well that could be a bit of a problem,' confessed Hermes. 'I established his whereabouts before I left Olympus but unfortunately he's not at his royal residence in the capital Sofia, but at some isolated private retreat he's built high in the Sredna Gora mountains in the centre of the country. I can only hope that he has an adequate court there; along with foreign spies; and telegraph lines that will allow our message to be quickly transmitted to all concerned.'

'But anyway,' he said, again consulting the bank of dials, 'I think we may have a bigger problem. According to this airspeed indicator we're travelling at barely 20 miles an hour. At this rate it would take us two days to get to Bulgaria and the invasions are all planned for tomorrow morning.'

'Well that's got to be it then,' said Heracles. 'Let's just go home and watch it all.'

Just then a gust of wind blew through the open cabin window scattering a sheath of loose log sheets around the enclosed compartment.

'Hi there fellers,' called a voice. 'What are you two doing up here ?'

Hermes and Heracles turned. They were no longer alone in the cabin. There stood a familiar figure, his huge wings filling the tiny compartment behind them, his stallion's mane of white hair framing his mature features and his strong manly body tappering into a pair of scaly lizard-like legs. It was Boreas, the North Wind.

'Consummate timing, my friend,' cried Hermes in relief. 'How did you find us ?'

'Not too difficult,' said Boreas. 'I've been keeping my eye on man's attempts to invade my realm recently and when I saw this contraption I thought I'd better come and investigate. I was just about to find out whether or not it would burn well in order to teach them for their arrogance but I didn't expect to find you two on board though.'

'Boreas,' said Hermes, 'I can't explain now but Heracles and I are on a mission for Zeus. Its vital that we get to the Balkans by dawn but we'll never make it in this thing at its current speed. Do you think you could whistle us up a tail wind that can get us there in time ?'

'Does Minos have asses ears, buddy ? Just leave it to me,' said the North Wind and he launched himself from the pod and disappeared behind the Zeppelin.

Presently the canvas on the airship began to flap violently as a strong wind built up. Eventually the whole frame of the Zeppelin became distorted and pushed forward. The steel frames creaked and groaned with the strain as the ship lurched forwards, propelled by the gale. The air speed indicator went over the top as the craft gathered speed.

Above the roar of the wind and the groaning of the airship frame Hermes called to Heracles, who was holding on tightly to a rail and looking a quite a little queasy. 'Fantastic,' he yelled. 'I reckon we're doing over a 100 miles an hour now. Provided the ship itself holds up we should make Bulgaria by sunrise.'

'Great,' said Heracles, as he recycled that morning's breakfast.

* * *

Chapter Thirteen

As he rounded Saint Catherine's Point on the southern tip of the island the sun was already starting to sink in the sky painting the sea ahead of him a glorious crimson gold. After a slow journey around the eastern perimeter Zeus finally picked up a little tail wind which filled his sail and propelled the tiny boat forward as he neared his destination.

Earlier Zeus had surveyed the countless battleships lying off Portsmouth as he left the Solent for the open English Channel. Before his little nap all sailors had relied on the gods of water, wind and the forest without whose favour they were helpless. But in the blink of an eye this had all changed. No more was the mighty oak a cherished national resource on which the very security of the nation rested. No longer need Admirals anxiously survey the sky and pray for a fair wind to lift their fleets from the doldrums. Now mankind gouged his strength from the raw earth; iron, coal and oil replacing the uncertainties of wood, wind and tide and giving mortals ever more power over their own destinies. Or at least that's how they felt it to be. In practise all destiny, whether for man or god, lay in the hands of Moros. All man had learned was how to blindly pursue an ever more destructive and violent route towards whatever Moros had in store for him.

As the little boat bobbed through the waves he saw before him a deep fissure in the cliff face. In earlier years smugglers in the dark of night had anchored off its rocky coast and rowed their cargoes of French brandy ashore to be hidden in the numerous caves. Now abandoned this chine had provided an ideal hideaway for the god of the sea from which to survey his handiwork. Zeus hoped that Hermes and Hera had been successful in preventing the English and French from going to war with each other. Time would soon tell but in the meantime he had a score to settle with his errant brother and that took priority over everything else.

Of sea, land or air Zeus had taken the curious and perhaps risky decision to approach this showdown from his brother's domain. He had decided this after careful consideration, hoping that Poseidon's preoccupation with the impending slaughter might lead him to ignore a lone yachtsman, giving Zeus time to land and block any retreat his brother might make towards the water. As the king of the gods scanned the cliff face for some sign of activity, from the depths of a dank cave a malign and care worn pair of eyes anxiously stared back at him.

Suddenly the waves ahead of him turned ominously black. Then the little boat was almost capsized as the water parted and the massive scaly green head of a sea monster reared up from below. The monster's neck extended above the mast of the boat. Two gleaming red eyes turned maliciously towards the craft and beneath flaring nostrils the creature's mouth parted to reveal its sabre-like rows of teeth.

Zeus and the monster stood eyeing each other for a second.

'You now know who I am,' he bellowed. 'Go back from whence you came.'

But the giant head came crashing down towards him. From out of a cloudless sky a mighty thunderbolt struck the creature's neck in mid thrust and it exploded in a shower of rank flesh as the sea about them crackled with the electric energy.

Zeus struggled with the boat to prevent it being sucked down beneath the waves as the monster's carcass sank from sight and he pointed the bow directly at the shore.

He could now see his adversary. Poseidon had broken cover and stood thirty feet tall above the cliff. The god of the sea lunged at the rock face with his trident splitting off a huge bolder which he grabbed with both hands, lifting it high above his head and then sending it roaring through the air towards the boat. As the rocky missile approached Zeus carefully manipulated the helm, deftly turning the small craft to avoid the rock as it came crashing down into the sea on his starboard side, nearly capsizing the boat once again with its splash.

Another bolder followed and then another. Three times the king of the gods skilfully dodged the missiles. The fourth shot came crashing down on the bow, ripping through the mast and shattering the brave craft into pieces. As the boat and its occupant disappeared beneath the waves from the cliff top Poseidon screamed out in triumph.

Overhead storm clouds were quickly filling the dusky sky that only moments earlier had been set fair. Then, as a thunderous rumble shock the earth, a gigantic figure slowly raised himself from the water and strode ashore. Zeus, himself now having assumed giant proportions, stood amongst the rocks and looked up at his brother towering over the cliff top above him. Around them the wind howled while thunder and lightning tore at the ever darkening sky.

'You cannot win,' he yelled above the tempest. 'There will be no war, no slaughter. The other gods have reared in the foolish mortals whom you would have fight for your sport. Submit now and return with me to Olympus unless you want to taste my fury.'

'You are wrong, brother,' called back Poseidon. 'My creatures tell me that everything is going ahead as planned. The mortals are poised to crash into each other above, below and on either shore of this very stretch of water. You cannot stop it now. Soon man will slaughter man on a scale previously undreamed of and as ever more souls sink to the depths of my domain so ever more will man raise his prayers to me.'

And with that he again split a huge rock from the cliff face with his trident and sent it crashing down the fissure towards Zeus.

The king of the gods didn't move as a mighty thunderbolt struck the bolder which exploded into a cascade of dust. Then the skies themselves appeared to open and rained down a furious barrage of fire and lightning about the figure on the cliff top. Slowly the cowed god of the sea was driven down the cliff face under the force of the barrage towards the terrifying figure waiting for him on the shore. Poseidon lost his footing and tumbled the remaining fifty feet with an avalanche of rubble to lie in a bruised and scorched heap beneath his tormentor.

'Now do you yield ?,' barked Zeus.

Poseidon's sad countenance looked up at his brother's stern face. He began slowly to rise to his feet and as he did so he transformed his shape. Zeus found himself now confronting a giant white stallion. Attempting to escape the stallion reared up and leapt to the left of the god towards the open sea but as he did Zeus reached out and grabbed its flowing mane, throwing himself up onto the creature's back and clinging to it as it sped out over the water.

Horse and rider galloped eastwards over the top of the crashing waves, whipped into a fury by the violent thunderstorms above. The horse reared and veered but could not shake off the rider fastened to its back. Finally it plunged deep beneath the waves and as the pair now sank to the sea bed Zeus found himself gripping the throat of a serpent, its coils entwining and squeezing his body.

For several minutes god and god-serpent grappled with each other beneath the waters of the English Channel. At last Poseidon's strength began to wane and his body resumed his normal form as he lie on his back with his brother's unbreakable grasp still pressing on his throat. Poseidon had one trick left.

The god of the sea, amongst his other attributes, was also the god of earthquakes. In a last desperate attempt to free himself Poseidon pounded the sea bed with his arms and legs. Slowly the booming vibrations resonated through the ground below them, building up until it began to shake and heave with a violent fury as the sea above them swirled like wine in a tossed goblet. Above that the thunder and lightning continued to tear the sky in its fury.

The pair were tossed about in an underwater maelstrom but nothing would shake Zeus's grip. The sea god's body went limp as the last of his strength drained from him and, slowly, the furious vibrations began to subside. The king of the gods had once again triumphed in a test of strength with his rebellious sibling.

Zeus dragged Poseidon's unconscious body back along the sea bed to the chine by Saint Catherine's Point, recovering along the way the special chains he had bought with him from the sunken wreckage of his yacht. Once on shore he bound the sea god securely to a rock deep inside a cave within the fissure and sealed its entrance with a huge bolder. He was confident that his brother would stay there safely out of harms way whilst he decided on a suitable punishment, even if it took a few hundred years to come up with something really worthy of Poseidon's villainy.

Well, it had been a long day. He thought he might as well cross the island and see if Hera had returned to Osborne House, hopefully with the news that she'd successfully made the English call off their planned invasion of France. He wondered how Hermes had been getting on in trying to stop the other five powers from going to war but that would have to wait until he got back to Olympus. Anyway, Ares was still on the lose somewhere and he'd need to be dealt with before this rebellion was properly bought under control.

* * *

Chapter Fourteen

After picking up the wide Danube glistening in the moonlight below them and following its course south at breakneck speed for most of the night the zeppelin conveying Hermes and Heracles had now veered eastwards with the river as the sun rose between the outstretched arms of the Transylvanian Alps to their north and the Balkan Mountains to their south, brilliantly reflecting off the marshy flatlands between the two ranges.

As they had crossed above the remote border lands between Serbia and Bulgaria they had spied from their vantage point in the sky the primitive roads clogged with Austrian soldiers, cavalry, artillery and wagons all heading in the same general direction as themselves. Now, lined up along the northern banks of the Danube, across the border with Rumania, they could make out the camps of the Russian army readying themselves to cross over and begin their own invasion of Bulgaria.

Hermes waved his hand through the right window of the cabin to signal to Boreas a slight change of direction and the gale from their west turned a little towards the south-east which, together with Hermes' rudder adjustments, pointed the airship away from the river and towards the eastern tip of the Balkan Mountains.

Finally, as the sun continued its relentless climb signalling to Hermes that time was running out fast, the mountains reared up below them and Boreas returned to the cabin.

'That's the place you're looking for,' said the North Wind, pointing towards a grim castle hacked into the side of a cliff.

'It looks pretty deserted and pretty remote to me,' said Hermes anxiously as he surveyed the relic from a bygone age below them. 'We'd better get down there and have a look around though. My information certainly suggests that this is where we're going to find Prince Ferdinand and he's still the only chance we've got of forestalling the Russian, Austrian and Turkish invasions which are getting underway this very minute.'

'I don't give a cyclops fart about any of them,' growled Heracles, who had been silent for most of the journey and had firmly resolved that flying was something strictly for the birds. 'Just you get this damned contraption down and me on the ground. I'll make my own way back to Olympus from here.'

'O.K. Hek, but after we've spoken to the Prince,' Hermes assured him.

'If he's even here,' said the grim giant. 'Otherwise I'm off.'

They circled the castle. A large square cobbled courtyard was surrounded by high stone walls and turrets where a single pair of mammoth wood and iron doors were bolted to an outside world connected to the fortress by a solitary, steep and narrow mountain path snaking out to the south. To the north the walls were cut deep into the mountainside itself where their iron grilled windows overlooked a sheer drop of thousands of feet. Heracles imagined the many poor wretches that must have been flung to their destiny through these portals by savage Balkan warlords over the preceding centuries.

'We can probably just about get this thing down in that courtyard,' said Hermes. 'I'll start slowly releasing gas, Boreas, if you can get out there and give us a few gentle breezes to guide us in. Heracles and I can take it from there; after all, you hardly look like a German army officer; so, thanks again for your help and we'll see you back at Olympus at the next council meeting.'

'Happy to be of help fellers. Good luck,' said the North Wind and he leapt from the cabin door.

With the aid of his personal wind Hermes had little difficulty in bringing the zeppelin smoothly down near filling the empty courtyard. When the craft had finally come to rest he leapt out to tether the lines and surveyed the scene around him. Heracles stumbled out, relieved to once more be on terra firma but finding his legs a little unsteady and his head dizzy.

'Doesn't seem to be a soul around,' he grumbled. 'Let's go home.'

Just then a door opened from buildings to the north end of the castle and a strange figure emerged garbed like some medieval servant. Straggly thinning strands of long white hair speckled a wart-encrusted head tapering into a long beak-like nose and a grimacing mouth lined with shark-like teeth. The twisted, hunchbacked little old man; if indeed man he was; slowly lurched towards the astonished pair.

'What do you want ?,' the varlet spat at them.

'We are emissaries from the Kaiser Wilhelm with an urgent message for Prince Ferdinand. Its vital that we see the Prince without delay,' replied Hermes. 'Is he here ?'

A wicked red eye with a glint in it looked up at him from the knarred creature. 'Oh, he's here all right,' he rasped. 'You better follow me, I'll find out if he'll see you,' and he gestured to them with a claw-like hand.

They were led into a large hall. It was exactly how you would expect to find the inside of a medieval castle. A huge log fire burned at one end beyond a rough wooden table. The cold stone floors and walls were decked with all manor of armour, swords, shields, lances, maces and myriad other implements from a bygone age of warfare. Not a thing in the room, including the servant, looked less than four hundred years old.

The creature went to the table and poured two silver goblets of dark red wine from an old clay jug.

'Gentlemen, please refresh yourselves while I tell the Prince you're here,' he said displaying a surprising charm and he shuffled off through a door at the rear of the hall.

They had neither ate nor drank since leaving Germany the previous afternoon and eagerly attacked the wine, Hermes insisting on his share as Heracles downed one goblet after another, helping himself to refills from the jug.

'I don't I like this at all, this just doesn't seem right somehow,' he said. 'It seems like we've gone back in time. And what do you make of that servant ? He reminds me of something, I just can't place what it is.'

'He looks to me more like one of those foul Keres than a mortal,' mumbled Heracles looking around the hall in a vain search for something to eat.

'That's it,' snapped Hermes. 'He is a Keres. A blood sucker from Hades. I thought I recognised the little bastard. But what in the name of Moros is he doing here. Oh no ! You know who the Keres serve ?'

Hermes looked up in horror at Heracles. Just then the hall started to spin around his head. He felt his senses leave him as he tumbled to the floor. From the far side of the room Heracles looked up from the cupboard he been rummaging about in, still searching for something to eat, to see his companion drop and suddenly his own head started swimming, his body reeled and his huge bulk came crashing down to the floor.

* * *

When Heracles came to he found himself in some huge, dim underground chamber. Rows of massive stone columns supported the roof and the whole vast area between the columns was piled high with countless wooden crates. He was naked and tethered to a central column by heavy iron chains. Opposite him he could see Hermes similarly bound and still unconscious. In a heap on the floor lay their German officers' uniforms and his briefcase.

Still groggy, he strained with all his strength against the chains, but to no avail. No mortal could fashion a bond strong enough to hold the god, these chains were the work of Hephaestus himself. He heard Hermes slowly murmuring back into life.

'So, little messenger, you join us,' laughed a deep voice. 'Struggle all you like, you great oaf, you will not break those bonds.'

They looked down the row of columns. At the end, on a stone throne set between two burning braziers fixed to the wall, sat a terrifying figure dressed in a full suit of battle armour. His dark eyes glowering at them from behind his helmet. They had finally found Ares.

'So you thought you could upset my plans, did you ?,' crowed the god of war. 'Well you've failed. By tonight all the nations of Europe will be at each other's throats in a war that will be like nothing that has gone before. Mortals will slaughter their fellow mortals in their millions and my Keres will drink of their blood on a thousand battlefields.'

'You're insane,' yelled Hermes at him. 'Do you really think Zeus is going to let you get away with this ?'

'Bah, Zeus. What do I care of Zeus,' scoffed Ares. 'War and nothing but war is about to reign supreme. Mankind will put their faith in me as they become ever more desperate for military victory over their enemies. But there'll be no quick relief in sight for them. Look about you, you fools. Those packing cases contain millions of tons of ammunition, firearms, shells, explosives and every conceivable weapon. From this isolated mountain fortress, which I've borrowed from the real Prince Ferdinand who is imprisoned elsewhere in the country, I can feed them enough armaments to keep them going for decades until the last drop of blood is drained from the last soldier.'

Hermes and Heracles both struggled against their chains, but it was in vain. There seemed nothing they could do. Hermes dropped his head in grief. He had failed in his mission. Even if Aphrodite and Zeus had managed, or even bothered, to prevent the western powers from going to war with each other there was nothing he could do to stop a war breaking out between Russia, Austria and Turkey, which would surely drag in the other powers quickly enough anyway.

'And now, my friends,' continued the god of war, 'you'd better try to make yourself comfortable because you're going to be spending quite a few years chained to those pillars as you watch these supplies slowly dwindle. But don't worry, this old castle is full of the most interesting devices designed long ago by mortals after my own heart. People who really knew how to extract a confession or two without shilly-shallying about. I've been itching to try my hand at some of these implements and I'm grateful to both of you for providing me with the opportunity to do so. Something to keep ourselves amused during the long winter nights. Now then, who wants to confess to something first ? Nobody got anything to confess to, eh ? Well we'll soon see about that.'

Ares plucked a branding iron from a coal brazier where it had been resting whilst he spoke. Its tip glowed white hot. Grasping it in his mailed fist he menacingly approached the captives.

'I think we'll start with this, ' he said. 'Crude, I grant you, but very effective.'

Through the stone chambers the chimes of a distant bell faintly echoed.

'Seven o'clock,' said the god of war. 'The Russian, Austrian and Turkish armies should just be entering Bulgaria about now. Don't worry though, they're not likely to come anywhere near this inaccessible hideaway to disturb our little games.

Just then the time bomb that von Schlieffen had placed in Heracles' briefcase exploded. In turn, the whole mountain exploded.

* * *

Chapter Fifteen

After his decisive victory over the Queen the Prime Minister, together with Chamberlain and Balfour, had travelled by train to Portsmouth in order to personally supervise the launch of the invasion of France. Everything seemed to be going according to plan now they had settled that unexpected little upset. By now troops would be starting to assemble at their staging posts ready to embark by midnight onto the specially commissioned fleet of barges that would convey them, under the protection of the Royal Navy, across the Channel for dawn landings at Dieppe. From the train window Salisbury contemplated the verdant Hampshire countryside glowing in the late afternoon sunlight of a glorious spring day.

'Perfect weather conditions,' he muttered to his companions.

They had been. But as the trio arrived at Portsmouth Naval Headquarters, as the evening sun was beginning to set, they could see the skies to their south from across the Solent and beyond the island starting to swirl with clouds and felt a light drizzle as they entered the building.

Along with the three leading members of the government the cream of the British military and political establishment had been gathered at Southsea Castle this evening. The fort provided the ideal point from which to view the launch of the invasion. Everything had been planned meticulously to the minute to co-ordinate this function with the activities going on outside. As the guests chatted over cocktails in the reception suite before sitting down to their five course meal one hundred thousand British troops would ready themselves at the makeshift jetties lining both banks of Southampton Water. At the same time the Royal Navy would be preparing to set sail from their moorings in Portsmouth Harbour. After the meal and preliminary speeches the Prime Minister was due to address the audience. It was actually during his speech that the order to sail would be given.

In a somewhat theatrical operation the Prime Minister's words would be transmitted by semaphore along the Solent to the waiting army and naval commanders. On this signal the troops would begin their embarkation and the fleet would set sail from Portsmouth. Under a moonlit sky the assembled elite would watch as the armada of small troop ships streamed out of the west towards them to be joined by their escort of battleships before sailing off to the east and south across the Channel and to a glorious victory that would settle once and for all the argument between Britain and France over who rules Africa.

As the Master of Ceremonies readied to call the guests to dinner Salisbury looked anxiously out of the window across the water. Violent thunderstorms now seemed to be pounding the southern tip of the Isle of Wight, although the weather outside still appeared to be fairly mild.

'I'm not sure I like the look of those storms,' he said turning to the First Sea Lord, Prince Louis Mountbatten. 'What d'you think ?'

'It looks pretty savage, I'll grant you,' said the Prince, 'but its by no means uncommon for isolated and brief storms to lash the south of the island. We've been watching the weather closely. Conditions here and elsewhere in the Channel look fine. That will probably soon blow itself out but I don't think we have anything to worry about at this stage.'

'I hope not,' said the Prime Minister, 'although we have contingency plans to postpone the invasion if necessary I'd hate to spoil tonight's entertainments.'

'I'm sure that won't be necessary,' said the Prince as they went in for dinner.

Over the hors d'oeuvres the storm to their south continued to rage but in a worrying development it appeared to be moving out at some speed eastwards and into the middle of the Channel; directly into the path of the invasion fleet. Over the meal Prince Louis had bobbed up and down to consult aides and now resumed his seat next to the Prime Minister as soup was served.

Balfour was just about to reach for the salt cellar when it moved about an inch to its left as if by its own volition. He darted his hand away in shock and stared at the object, now quite still. Thinking he must have imagined it he reached for the cellar again. And as he did it moved again.

'Uncle,' he said, feeling a little foolish, 'that salt cellar keeps moving.'

'Not now, Arthur,' snapped Salisbury. 'Now Louis, what's the latest ? I said I didn't like the look of that storm. Something just doesn't feel right about it.'

'It's still very localised, Robert,' said the First Sea Lord. 'and it appears to be moving east at a great speed. Its out over the Channel at the moment but if it continues on its present course it will be over Holland long before our fleet is out into the open sea. Elsewhere everything remains calm and the thing must blow itself out soon. I assure you there is nothing to worry about.'

He had no sooner finished his words when a deep rumble suddenly welled up from the rocks beneath them on which the fortress was built. The windows rattled, cutlery on the tables tinkled against glasses, the soup in the bowls in front of them started to swirl and Balfour let out a yelp as this time the salt cellar he had just plucked up the courage to reach for again moved a full foot across the table.

For several minutes the rumbling continued. Those in the room sat frozen to their seats staring at each other and wondering what was happening to them, few of those present ever having experienced an earthquake before. Finally the vibrations began to subside.

'What in God's name ?,' was all Salisbury could stutter.

The roast beef course now forgotten most rushed to the windows to look outside whilst those who did recognise an earthquake when they were in one, even an apparently mild and far off one, instead rushed to the exits.

The building was now still but the sea outside was churning violently. To their east they could hear a strange distant sound. At first a low, almost indiscernible, drone building in intensity as if something were approaching them. And then they saw it.

A wall of water stretching between the eastern tip of the island and the southern shore of the mainland was racing towards them. As they stood transfixed the tsunami washed over and through them, shattering the windows and filling the banqueting hall like a goldfish bowl, before continuing its course up the Solent.

As the water subsided the dazed and drenched politicians, admirals, generals, lords and ladies slowly gathered themselves amidst the upturned tables and debris of the flooded hall. Balfour lay unconscious in a corner, a soup bowl having found its way onto his head and a large cod having buried itself in the front of his waist coat. Sea slime covered the bushy white beard of the Prime Minister as he righted himself and looked about him in disbelief.

The fleet in the shelter of Portsmouth Harbour took a battering but survived the ordeal. Less lucky were the hundreds of tiny wooden barges lined up along the more exposed Southampton Water. They and their jetties were reduced to so much driftwood by the freak wave. An hour or two later and the empty boats would have been jam packed with British soldiers, most of whom fortunately escaped with no more than a drenching.

There could be no question left. Without the barges that had been carefully prepared and assembled for this moment there was no effective means of transporting the army across the Channel. The British invasion of France was not simply to be postponed. This calamity meant that it would need to be cancelled indefinitely.

* * *

The lantern lights flickered and cast countless dancing shadows that rippled down through the rough circular walls of the tunnel giving the impression of watching a caterpillar move from inside its belly. Chief Engineer Marcel Blanc proudly completed his final inspection of his masterpiece. Just seven months after the start of drilling, using his revolutionary new steam driven boring machine, the tunnel under the English Channel had been completed right on schedule.

In a short while Marcel would stand proudly beside the President and the other VIPs as they watched the columns of French soldiers file into the tunnel mouth to begin an eight hour march which would see them emerge at dawn in the Kent countryside. From a remote barn, carefully prepared by French agents to conceal the tunnel exit, an entire French army would emerge complete with cavalry and artillery support catching the English, who had always relied on their naval power to defend their island from invasion, totally by surprise. By the following morning London itself should be in the hands of the occupying French forces and the score would be finally be settled for Fashoda and a hundred other indignities inflicted on La France by the arrogant English.

Alone with his thoughts in the dim candle lit tunnel Marcel was swept by an almost religious-like ecstasy. This construction was his crowning achievement. The love and the passion of his life. And now as he stood in its deep cavern its very walls seemed to groan and heave with delight as he now consummated his date with destiny. In fact, they really did seem to be groaning and heaving.

Coming to his senses Marcel realised something was wrong. The ground beneath his feet was shaking. The groaning was actually coming from the rock walls of the tunnel grinding together against themselves. Down the length of the tunnel away into the darkness the whole thing seemed to be twisting and curling like a snake.

'Sacre Bleu,' he uttered, 'what is happening ?'

He felt a drip of water splash on his head. For an instant it didn't register. Then the terrible realisation of what that might mean began to fight its way into his brain.'

'No, no. Don't let it be,' he sobbed, and he turned his lantern to look up at the tunnel roof.

From numerous tiny fissures that were appearing in the rock water was slowly starting to drip. A few splashes at first. Then more. Then a tiny piece of rock would break away and the dripping would become a spurt of water. The length of the tunnel water was seeping in and starting to collect in puddles on the tunnel floor.

'MERDE,' he yelled and ran for his life in the direction of the tunnel entrance.

* * *

President Loubet cast his eyes around the fields full of French soldiers as he and his entourage mounted the podium that had been erected alongside the tunnel entrance at a French chateau near Calais. The structures concealing the entrance had now been removed and both it and the podium were draped in tricolour flags and rosettes. Soon he would give the order to march and he would stand proudly over his brave men as they filed, in perfect order, into the dark orifice on their historic mission. He, Emile Loubet, was about to achieve what every ruler of France, even Bonapart himself, had only been able to dream about. The invasion of England.

'Vive La France,' he would yell in encouragement to the troops as they passed by.

'Vive Loubet,' they would yell back. Such ecstasy.

'Well, when can we get started ?,' he impatiently demanded of the Chief of Staff.

'The Chief Engineer is just completing his final inspection of the tunnel, Monsieur President,' replied the General. 'He should be back any moment.'

As if on cue the Chief Engineer emerged. Running out of the tunnel entrance as fast as his legs would carry him, arms outstretched and his contorted face as white as chalk.

'It's leaking, it's leaking!,' he screamed.

'What did he say ?,' asked Loubet, and they turned to look at the tunnel entrance before them.

As they did the tunnel instead became a giant hosepipe as a column of salt water ten feet in diameter burst from its entrance, smashing into the podium and sweeping it, together with its occupants, away into the nearby fields crammed with the waiting formations of soldiers. For some time the torrent continued, like a gigantic waterspout drenching the entire army until finally it stopped leaving a mass of confused bodies wallowing in the now marshy fields.

Loubet's bruised body lay face down in the mud some hundreds of yards from the tunnel entrance where he'd started. His smart uniform was covered in mud and he'd lost his beautiful cockaded hat. As he lifted his head he could see all around him soggy, muddy and battered French generals and other dignitaries slowly coming round, being helped here and there by equally disordered troops. He had no way of knowing, nor would he ever know, that at about this very time across the Channel the cream of the English establishment were contemplating a similarly damp and indignant end to their own ambitions of military glory.

President Loubet wept.

* * *

On the morning of the 1st April Kaiser Wilhelm II sat unsteadily on his mount flanked by the lines of Junkers, the Prussian military aristocracy, reviewing the massed ranks of the German special forces ready, on his orders, to stream across the nearby Belgium border and then sweep down the poorly defended French Channel coast, cutting off any aide from England and encircling Paris. Simultaneously the orders would be transmitted mobilising the entire German armed forces to resist any French counter attack in the south and reinforce the spearheading assault.

Mercifully the traitor Hans Job had not managed to escape with the real mobilisation plans. The train journey west had been an unpleasant one for Wilhelm, who had been deeply humiliated by having to stand by and watch whilst his personal favourite had stolen Germany's most prized secret weapon. The Kaiser had dined alone and then consoled himself with not a little French brandy which he was now feeling the effects of. He knew he shouldn't, but he couldn't help but take some consolation from Von Schliffen's confident assurances that the zeppelin and its occupants would soon be captured inside German territory. No word had been heard of either since the craft had been observed crossing over the Austro-Hungarian border at dusk. So at least Wilhelm wasn't the only one who'd got things wrong and he would make a point of not letting them forget it.

This though had also tended to support the theory that Hans was in fact an Austrian, or perhaps a Russian, spy interested only in the zeppelin rather than working for the French and that their imminent invasion plans were thus likely unthreatened. Von Schliffen had been consulting with the military intelligence officers and was now due to give Wilhelm his final report prior to the Kaiser issuing the order to march. Presently Wilhelm saw him and his staff riding towards them.

The party of Generals drew up in front of the Kaiser and his nobles. Von Schlieffen and the rest all looked decidedly uneasy about something and he seemed to be having some difficulty in getting his words out.

'Well,' growled Wilhelm finally, 'what's the verdict ?'

'Kaiser,' said Von Schlieffen, 'I don't quite know how to tell you this. We've been receiving reports overnight from our agents inside French territory. We've checked and re-checked and all the reports we're getting are confirming them same thing. Its unbelievable, Your Majesty, I just can't think how they knew.'

'What's unbelievable. Who knew what ?,' demanded Wilhelm. 'What in the devil are you blathering about ?'

'Kaiser,' said Von Schlieffen gravely, stiffening to attention in his saddle, 'the whole of Flanders seems to be teeming with the French army. We expected the French to be in their normal positions along our borders in Alsace and Lorraine. Instead they're ready and waiting smack bang in the path of our planned invasion. I don't know how, but somehow the traitor Hans Job must have discovered and revealed our plans to them. That's the only explanation. Your Majesty, we can't possibly proceed with the limited forces at our disposal. We have been betrayed and, at least for the moment, we must call the invasion off.'

Wilhelm sat for some minutes taking in what the Chief of Staff had just told him. It had been a period of non stop disappointment. First Hans' betrayal and the loss of the zeppelin. Now this further humiliation in front of the assembled ranks of the German ruling class.

'We better all go home then,' was all he could finally bring himself to say meekly.

Just then, as if to add to their gloom, a playful cloud burst forth a torrential downpour.

* * *

Chapter Sixteen

Dawn broke with a chorus of bugle calls summoning the Russian soldiers from their tents along the marshy northern banks of the Danube that separated Rumania from Bulgaria. A flotilla of boats stood waiting to ferry the troops across the wide river to begin their invasion of the, nominally, Turkish principality.

The Tsar himself had secretly travelled to this isolated frontier to personally issue the orders to proceed. As he rode with his splendid retinue of officers and advisors and reviewed his massive army readying itself on this fine spring morning he felt supremely confident in the success of his mission. Before Turkey and the rest of the world even knew what was happening his forces would have overrun Bulgaria and be massing on its southern border little more than a day's march from Constantinople. The Black Sea was about to become a truly Russian lake. Russian guns would guard the Bosporus and the Dardanelles and Mother Russia would at last have her access to the waters of the Mediterranean, so long denied her by the other Great Powers.

All his closest advisors; the military, the politicians and the astrologers; were all in agreement. Nothing could go wrong to spoil his plans. The Tsar and his party dismounted at his headquarters tent for breakfast and a final consultation whilst they watched the troops begin their embarkation.

Little did they know that less than a hundred miles to their south-west a similar scene was taking place in the mountainous borderland between Serbia and Bulgaria as the old Austrian Emperor, who had also insisted on making the arduous journey in order to launch his own invasion plans, dipped his toast soldiers into his boiled egg and watched his real soldiers rousing themselves to begin an adventure that would restore the greatness of the Hapsburg Empire.

A strange event was about to unite the two.

As the Tsar and his advisors poured over maps of the rough Bulgarian terrain laid out on a table in front of his tent they noticed some consternation amongst the nearby troops. The men were looking at and pointing to something in the sky. Those officers with field glasses and telescopes were all training them in the same direction.

'What's going on ?,' insisted the Tsar to an aide.

Training his binoculars the Colonel gasped in amazement. 'Your Majesty,' he stammered, 'I'm not sure what it is. Its something in the sky. And it seems to be moving at a phenomenal speed.'

'Whatttt ?,' came the collective response and they all rushed forward to view the object.

Sure enough, streaking across the sky to their west was a huge black cigar-shaped object, now turning away from the river and heading directly into Bulgaria.

'What in heaven's name is that ?,' asked the Tsar in amazement. He was greeted with silence. No one had the faintest idea.

They continued to stare at the craft as it speed off towards the eastern tip of the Balkan mountain range stretching out along the far southern horizon. Through their telescopes they eventually observed the now distant dot come to a halt above a mountain peak and slowly descend out of sight.

The Tsar's earlier confidence had now been shattered and his natural tendency towards superstition and anxiety was starting to reassert itself. 'What is it. What does it mean ?,' he asked nervously glancing around his court of soldiers and seers. Throughout the distant ranks of soldiers small groups huddled together mumbling discontentedly about evil omens in the sky.

After a brief exchange with his officers General Kuropatkin, the Minister of War, finally said, 'Your Majesty, this could be very serious. The object may have been an airship. Various engineers and nations have been trying to develop such a machine but nothing like this has even been remotely dreamed of. The speed of the craft alone defies any scientific explanation.'

'Then what is it. Where's it come from ?,' insisted the Tsar.

'Majesty, I know what it is,' boomed out a deep, sombre voice. All eyes turned towards Grigorie, the former vagabond monk who was now the Tsar's personal holy man and spiritual advisor. An unholy fraudster in the eyes of many assembled there but they had no choice but to humour him or doubt his influence over Nicholas.

'They've come. I always knew they'd come,' intoned the monk.

'Who's come ?,' squealed the Tsar.

'The men from Mars,' replied Grigorie gravely. 'This is Armageddon. The end of the world.'

'That's ludicrous,' demanded the General. 'Men from Mars indeed. Your Majesty, there has to be a more down to earth explanation for this object.'

'No, no,' quipped in a young scientific advisor, 'he's right. You said yourself. No nation on Earth has a workable flying machine let alone anything capable of the speeds of that craft. And what's it doing here. The thing has got to have come from another planet. Your Majesty, we could be witnessing the beginning of an invasion of the Earth.'

Nicholas was by now fast becoming a quivering wreck. 'What are we going to do ?,' he pleaded.

'Your Majesty,' insisted General Kuropatkin, 'We cannot afford to let ourselves get carried away with all this nonsense about men from Mars invading the Earth. Look at them. We have one hundred thousand ignorant and superstitious soldiers who have already been unnerved by this object. We risk wholesale panic breaking out if we let these rumours spread. There has to be a simpler explanation. All right, we've seen something strange in the sky. Perhaps it was some sort of optical illusion. I'd certainly want to see a little more evidence than that before I was ready to believe the Earth was being invaded from outer space.'

The General didn't have to wait long. As a thousand telescopes and binoculars continued to peer at the distant mountain where the craft had disappeared they watched in awe as the entire peak lifted itself into the sky under the influence of some unimaginable explosive force. Minutes passed before the thunderous shock wave of the explosion reached them, shaking the ground like an earthquake.

'Satisfied now ?,' said the smug scientist.

'My God. My God,' was all the General could say. The Tsar was dumbstruck. Terror filled the faces of the Russian troops who would now be more likely to obey an order to invade hell than they would be to march towards the scene of such devastating power.

'We must call off the planned invasion and return home immediately,' said Kuropatkin finally. 'This could be the end of the human race if we're being invaded by Martians equipped with flying bombs that can destroy entire mountains. My God, just think what they could do to an army, or a city.'

In not too good order the Russian army that little more than an hour earlier had been ready to march on Constantinople hurriedly packed their equipment and set off on the long journey back to Moscow.

From the moment they too had observed the strange craft streaking across the skies above them a similar drama had unfolded in the Austrian camp, although their scientific advisors thought it more likely that Venusians, rather than Martians, were responsible for the devastating demonstration of power they had witnessed. Confusion and panic had broken out as the troops fought for access to the narrow roads that would lead them back to Vienna.

Far to the south, beyond the Balkan mountains, things had been going better for the Turkish 3rd Army of Macedonia as it picked its way into Bulgarian territory without yet encountering any local opposition. Shielded by the mountains they hadn't observed the zeppelin. They couldn't, however, miss the explosion. As the debris rained down from the skies all order dissolved. The poorly trained, poorly paid and poorly led soldiers simply dropped their weapons, abandoned their equipment and ran as fast as they could back across their own border.

Epilogue

Heracles and Hermes eventually dug themselves out of the rubble and dragged the defeated God of War back to Olympus in Hephaestus' chains. There Zeus had him tethered to the mountainside, leaving Poseidon similarly chained in his cave on the Isle of Wight whilst he decided on some longer term punishment. Zeus beamed benignly on the other gods and goddesses congratulating them all on their fine work in preventing the Great Powers of Europe from plunging into war with each other. The Olympians returned to their lives of idle luxury and the pursuit of pleasure.

Zeus surveyed the scene below him from the sacred pool. From Paris to St Petersburg, from London to Berlin, Europeans everywhere basked in the sunshine of a balmy summer's afternoon with thoughts of war far from their minds. It was a continent at peace with itself at the start of a beautiful new age. An age in which the march of science, art and enlightenment would shine a bounty of peace, prosperity and progress on its happy people.

'All seems to be well down there,' said a smiling King of the Gods looking up at his faithful messenger. 'There shouldn't be any trouble now for at least a hundred years. I think I'll have a little nap.'

In some place unfathomable to both gods and man Moros, who held all their fates in his hand, smiled a grim smile.

End

Printed in Great Britain
by Amazon.co.uk, Ltd.,
Marston Gate.